EVERY HEART

By LK Collins

DEDICATION

★ ★ ★

For my Father, thank you for always loving me and supporting me.

PROLOGUE

-Nate-

"How are you feeling?" a nurse asks me.

Looking around the desolate hospital room, that's a loaded question.

"I'm not sure how to answer that."

"Physically, Mr. Wilcox?" she asks in her thick, German accent.

"I'm okay, better than I've been for about the last year."

"Good, well, keep resting. You're healing well. Your family should be here any time."

Looking at her long, blonde hair as she leaves the room, it reminds me of Arion. I can't help but feel happy, knowing soon she'll be here. I've been waiting so long to see her, to hear her voice, to touch her. Finally, today is that day. My eyes are heavy...I'm still so tired all the time and don't have the strength to do much. So I take the nurse's advice and close them, envisioning my parents and *my girl*.

Soon, I'm awakened by a familiar touch and a voice I know all too well. Smiling to myself, I open my eyes to see both of my parents. They're crying, looking down at me, and it kills me that my decisions have done this to them and our family.

"Oh, Nate," my mom says basically throwing herself at me. Reaching up despite my weakness, I wrap an arm around her. Feeling her again brings tears to my eyes. Glancing at my dad, he has a hand on my arm, red faced, and is just staring at me. I reach for his hand, and am so grateful that they are here. They traveled halfway across the world to be with me. Closing my eyes, I take everything in. But one person is missing.

Arion is not with them and as my mom pulls away, I can't help but watch the door, waiting for her to come running to me. "How are you?" my dad asks me, leaning down to hug me.

"I'm better, but still feeling pretty rough."

"You're so skinny," my mom says, gripping my hand.

"I know, Ma."

"But you're alive, and that's all that matters."

"Yes, it is," my dad adds. Pulling one of my hands away for a brief second, I wipe my eyes.

"How much do you know?" I ask them, wondering how forthcoming the military was with giving them information.

"We didn't know anything 'til we landed. On the drive over here, they told us what you've been through. I'm so sorry, Nate."

"It's okay, Dad, I survived. Only for you guys and Arion."

Bringing up her name puts a cloud over the room. I can tell both of my parents' attitudes change right away. They glance at each other, then nervously look around the room like the hospital equipment is interesting. They are looking everywhere except at me.

"Where is she?" I ask point blank, not able to stand it any longer that she hasn't come through the door.

"I'm sorry. She's not coming, son," my dad says.

Both and pain take over, almost crippling me, as I run through all of the reasons why she might not be here. My chest tightens and I ask, "Did something happen to her?"

"Oh God, no," my mom blurts out. "She's

okay, Nate, it's just…"

She trails off without finishing her sentence and puts her head down. I look at my dad hoping for the answers. I need to know why in God's name my fiancée isn't here.

"Dad?" I ask in a pleading tone after he doesn't say anything. I'm about to beg him to tell me when he says the worst words in the world.

"She's moved on, son," he says with tears in his eyes.

Agony takes over, almost paralyzing my heart. Never in a million years did I dream of hearing the news that she moved on. Never. Day in and day out, being chained like a pig and the thought never crossed my mind. Tears spill over and I look between my parents, my vision blurred.

"Why?" I ask, clenching my jaw.

My dad pulls a chair up and sits next to me. "She thought you were dead. The military told us long ago that you died in a roadside bombing."

"Will you excuse me?" my mom asks and gets up from the chair she's sitting in.

My dad asks her, "Are you okay, honey?"

She nods her head and walks away. I notice how frail she is and she's using a cane. "What's wrong with Mom?" I ask my dad, immediately alarmed.

"She has a lot of things going on right now, Nate."

"What the fuck does that mean?" I ask him, panicked.

"We wanted to wait to tell you, 'til you were feeling stronger."

"No, Dad, tell me now."

"I'm afraid your mother's been dealing with some serious health issues."

"Like what? Just tell me dammit," I say aggravated that he won't let me in on what's going on with my mom. "I can handle it."

"It's a lot to take in, so don't freak out. As of now, she's been diagnosed with MS and Aplastic Anemia, which is a rare blood disorder."

"Oh my God, what does that mean?" I ask whispering.

"She has a long road ahead of her, son. I don't think at this point with either of the diseases that the doctors can predict how her future will be."

I rest my head back against the pillow, my physical pain now replaced with anger. Arion's gone. My mom is dying. Why the fuck did I even bother surviving? What the fuck has happened? This is the exact opposite of what I was expecting. Closing my eyes, I know I have to fix this.

CHAPTER 1

-Nate-

Being in the hallway of her building and waiting for her to arrive is surreal. My body is flooded with emotions. I'm not sure how I'll respond when I see her, or how she will when she sees me. I don't know why I'm so worried. I know she will run to me. She has to. Arion is mine – she always has been and always will be. I mean, I love her enough to have stayed away for as long as I have, but not any longer...I need her.

I've dreamt of this moment a million times and imagined it going so many different ways. I wish I could scoop her up in my arms and carry her away. But I won't 'til she tells me she wants me and she's ready to leave him. Right now, she's not my girl and I know that. The thought alone fills my body with anger. She's moved on and really...I can't blame her, she thought I was dead. When you love someone the way I love her, you respect them even if it kills you in the process. I know for her to be living with someone, she must care deeply for him. And sometimes I wonder if it would be better if she thought I was still dead. She has a new life after all, and what place do I have in it? But my heart has been pulling me towards her and telling me that everything she has with this guy will wash away the moment she sees me.

I could blame me being here on my mom being sick. Arion needs to know what's going on with her, and neither of my parents are going to bear the bad news to her, but knowing Arion the way that I do, she would want to know. That's another reason why it pains me to have stayed away from her as long as I have.

Suddenly, my heart drops to the pit of my stomach. There she is. She's even more beautiful than I remember. She is the essence of flawlessness. More perfect than any other human being.

Staying back in the shadow of the hallway, I watch her look for something in her purse. I'm lost. It takes me a moment to snap out of it. I should help her with her groceries, but sadly…I can't, as I stand here on my crutches with more injuries than I'd like to name. I'm not the same man I once was, but what is the same: my love.

Finally, I will myself to move, close enough just to smell her scent. It's exactly as it was the day I left. The same smell I remember as I tucked my nose deep into her hair and said goodbye. That was the day I made the biggest mistake of my life.

She slides the key in the door and I know I have to stop her, so I reach for her. "A," I whisper, searching for the strength that's suddenly been stripped away. Her body tenses and I see a chill run over her as goose bumps form on her skin. It takes her a moment before she turns towards me. I stand frozen, trying to read her reaction. I won't push myself on her. She will come to me, I know she will.

Arion's skin turns pale, as if she's staring at a ghost. Considering what I've been through, being beaten, tortured, and starved, I should be a ghost. All of the grocery bags fall from her hands. The second the milk hits the floor, it busts open, tipping over and pooling at her feet. She takes her hands and presses them to the sides of her face, just shaking her head vigorously. *Dammit, this is not the reaction I wanted.* She looks terrified, like I'm a monster.

"Nate?" she questions. Like it's not really me standing before her.

Reaching for her to provide some sort of comfort, I say, "It's me, A."

She pulls away from me, the gesture a swift kick to the gut. *No, don't do that.* I dreamt of her running into my arms and now...this. Looking at her as tears roll down her cheeks, she just continues to shake her head and backs away from me 'til finally she's pressed firmly against the door. I don't want to scare her any more than I already have so I stay where I am, praying she comes to her senses and to me.

"Please, A, say something?"

"I...This...It's just a...dream...a dream. Wake up, Arion," she tells herself.

In the distance, I hear the elevator ping and we both turn to look down the hall. That's him and I know it. I've seen this asshole she's with on TV and shit. The basketball star himself. She starts to breathe heavily and reaches her hand for him as he walks down the hall. He takes in the scene, then runs to her and asks, "What's wrong, baby?"

He glances at me briefly, I know not making

the correlation yet. All he sees is her panicked and struggling to breathe.

"Nate," she whispers between deep, struggled breaths and looks at me. His head whips towards me and anger looms in his eyes. I know he can't believe it probably even more than she can't. Her gasping starts to get out of control and she moves her hand to her chest. "I can't breathe," she tells him.

"It's okay, baby, everything is going to be okay," he tells her holding on to her shoulders and looking into her eyes. Then all the color drains from Arion's face. Her eyes roll back into her head and she collapses. My instincts move me and I try to catch her, but my crutches slip on the milk and I hit the floor. I keep my eyes on her and Bain has her. I couldn't care less about me. I only watch her head, making sure it doesn't hit anything.

Holding it gracefully, Bain lays her down gently, cradling her head in his lap and shouts, "Baby? Baby, wake up." She doesn't respond and he looks at me and asks, "What the fuck happened, motherfucker?"

I shake my head, unsure how to answer his question. This is not something that I ever imagined in a million years. Leaning over her, he caresses her face and talks to her, coaxing her to wake up. "Come on, baby, wake up." She doesn't move, except for the slow breaths moving in and out of her. "Call 911," he orders.

"I don't have a phone," I respond, embarrassed, and scoot away to collect my crutches.

"How do you not have a phone?" he snarls at me angrily and calls himself. As I go to stand, he looks at my pants where the fabric is bunched at the spot where I lost the lower half of my leg.

Right away, I can tell that the wheels in his head are spinning. Then Arion begins to move and I can't stop myself from crawling to her. Looking at her, I want to touch her, to see if I can soothe her pain in any way. But Bain stares at me like a protective animal that's about to take his prey down, all the while giving the dispatcher her symptoms. While I just sit and shake my head, wanting to run my hand over her soft skin, wanting to be the one on the phone, wanting to be the one she reached for. But I'm not.

He hangs up and looks at me without saying anything. I mean, in a moment like this, what is there to say? Taking his eyes off of mine, he looks down and we both watch her. A lonely tear of his lands on her neck. He wipes it away and shakes his head. Being this close to her and not able to do anything kills me. Glancing up, I catch sight at the way he's looking at her and I know he loves her just as much as I do. I never dreamt of having competition for the woman I love when I was rescued. All I thought about was finally being able to be with Arion. I survived for one reason. One – her. Now, all of that is in jeopardy and I just don't know what to do.

The paramedics arrive rushing down the hall. Right away Bain stands up and moves out of their way, and I myself struggle a little more trying to get up. Surprisingly, Bain helps me up, then he hands me my crutches as I balance on my one leg. The paramedics begin to work on her, checking vitals and asking us what happened. Bain speaks, and I let him. Once they finally get her awake, they talk to her, asking all sorts of questions, but she is dazed and still really out of it. Her eyes are glazed over as she turns and looks at me. They move her onto a body board and start to strap her down, the sound of the Velcro instantly triggers a flashback…

"He's alive," a man shouts.

Slowly I move my head, trying to open my eyes. It's

the first time I've heard the voice of another person in almost two weeks. Why won't my eyes open? I can't see anything. I try to lift my arm to wipe away the dirt and grime that covers them and I remember how bad it hurts when I move.

I freeze from the pain. I should have been dead days ago, but...I'm not. I know the only reason is because of the small water leak coming from the ceiling. It drips a few drops here and there, and up until I couldn't see, I could catch them in my mouth.

"Man, you're fucking mental. He's dead," another man says.

I know this is my last chance at survival. Since I was left for dead, these are the first people I've encountered. I moan and try to move with every ounce of strength I have. It's excruciating, but I have to. They both stop talking as they catch my movement, then shout, "We've got a live one!"

"Stay still," one of them says and touches my shoulder. Then I feel a hand on my wrist.

"His pulse is weak and by the look of him, we'll need to airlift him out of here."

"Just hang in there, man, you're going to be okay."

I don't respond, I just lie still.

"I'm going to pour some water over your eyes, okay?"

I nod my head and then almost cry from the burning

sensation. They keep pouring water over and over, but still I can't see. Fuck, I'm blind.

"We're gonna get you out of here." They lift my weakened, emaciated body and the movement causes me to scream out in pain. My body trembles and my breathing is beginning to get so fast I fear I might pass out. But before darkness takes over, the last thing I remember loud and clear is the sound of Velcro as my body is tied down to a bodyboard...

The noise that day is exactly the same as it is now, watching Arion being secured for transport.

"Is one of you her significant other?"

"I am," Bain responds looking right at me. I nod my head, letting him know that I agree. The truth is, I am *not* hers, nor is she mine. Not now. I left her and made the biggest mistake the day I enlisted. Today I'd thought our love was strong enough and she would come running to me, but I guess not. Staring down at the ground, I can't bring my eyes up to meet his again.

The room is dark and everything is quiet, it's the only place that I feel at peace...alone and away from the world. For so many months, I laid like this, praying for the day that I would get to come home and see my family. My parents and Arion are all that really matter to me. They always have been and I know that will never change. Even if things with Arion didn't go as planned, I will never give up on her, because I was given a second chance at life, and I know my life was meant to be spent with her.

Even though I lived through hell, I knew the day my parents arrived in Germany at the military hospital and Arion did not come with them that something was wrong. But even then, I never gave up hope. Until now.

I should be thankful for being given a second chance at all, but how can I when the person who matters most to me, who kept me alive, day in and day out while I was living in hell, loves someone else?

Closing my eyes, I can still hear my dad's words as he broke the news to me. *She's moved on.* Both of my parents felt so sorry for me then, and they still do now. But sorry didn't do shit then and it sure as hell isn't doing shit now.

There's a knock on my door and I don't answer, instead I pretend that I'm sleeping like I have so many other times. My dad flips the light on and sits on my bed. "How are you holding up?"

I shake my head without responding.

"Listen, I know you're in pain and I feel for you, Nate, I really do. But dammit you're alive. Do you have any idea how lucky you are?"

"Trust me, Dad, I know," I gripe.

"Then would you start acting like it?"

Seriously? "Is this really how you're going to treat me? After thinking I was dead?"

"Nate, you know your mother is ill and you don't seem to give two shits about her or me for that fact. So yeah, this is how I'm going to treat you. You have a doctor's appointment in about an hour. Maybe you could shower and not act like your life is over. Open your eyes – you've been given an amazing second chance at life, son."

My dad walks off and I roll over, forcing myself to open my eyes. It hurts, fuck it hurts, but his words resonate with me. My mother is in a lot of pain and has taken the news of her medical problems really hard. Plus, as much as I don't want to admit it and want to wallow in my own bullshit...I *am* very lucky to be alive.

Thinking for a few moments about my parents, and what they must have gone through when I was gone…it's hard to even imagine…so I take a dose of my dad's advice, knowing I have to fake it for them. *I can do that.* They deserve at least that from me, not this pathetic immature person who sulks around. Plus, I need to figure out a plan to get Arion back. Being depressed and in bed isn't the place to do that.

Getting out of bed, I make my way into the bathroom, crutches and all. Leaning over, I turn the shower on and then sit on the lid of the toilet to get undressed. What used to be such a normal everyday thing is now so difficult. I become frustrated very easily, but do my best in this moment to keep that in check. Getting into the shower, I leave my crutches outside and sit on the stool that my dad put in here for me. Looking down at my legs, tears fill my eyes. It pains me to remember how I used to be. I was so athletic and full of energy.

When I left two years ago, I had so many plans and now…this is my reality. I guess it was crazy of me to think Arion wouldn't get on with her life after the news of my death. She's perfect and Bain jumped at the opportunity, now he's the lucky one.

I wipe away the tears, remembering my dad's words again. I begin to wash myself, trying to forget about everything for a little bit. I just want some relief from the torture of my mind. But then her face flashes before mine as I rinse myself. I think the thing that really sickens me most about it all is how when I showed up at her apartment, her reaction to me was that of...fear.

I should have stayed away like I'd planned, until I had my prosthetic and gained some weight, and maybe when Bain was out of town at a game. But I had too much time on my hands and it drove me mad not to be with her or have her, since I was back home and so close. So finally when I couldn't bear it any longer, I broke my own rules. I was becoming obsessed with needing to see her and had this vision that the moment she saw me, she would run into my arms and everything would be as it was.

Instead, my biggest fear came true and things went the complete opposite. I acted on a whim like I have so many other times, just took a cab to her place after I stumbled upon her address after searching and searching about her online.

She'd just moved into this elegant sky-rise

with an NBA player, but none of that mattered to me. I just needed to see my girl. It didn't make a difference that the military and the government asked that my return be kept low profile, for the chance they could find my captors before they knew I'd been found alive. I went against them too and made another mistake.

Now I don't have a clue what's going on with Arion. Is she okay? What's she thinking now that she knows I'm alive?

Getting out of the shower, I wrap a towel around my waist and stare at my reflection in the mirror. I look nothing like I used to. I can't gain weight, and I know it's because I never feel like eating, even though I know I have to. I used to think about food all the time when I was held captive, so I should be eating like a pig, but I just can't. I've lost the will to do anything for myself.

After I'm dressed and done getting ready, I head into the living room. My mom is on the couch and the second she sees me, she gets up with her cane assisting her.

"Ma, just stay sitting, will ya?"

"She's coming with us," my dad says as he rests his hands on both of our shoulders.

"You should stay home and rest, Ma."

"That's nonsense, dear, I've been without you for far too long. I'm coming along, end of story," my mom tells me with a firm, loving voice.

CHAPTER 2

-Bain-

To say that these last two days have been the scariest I've experienced since losing Kinsey would be an understatement. It's been total and brutal hell. Leaning my head on the edge of Arion's hospital bed, I watch her sleep peacefully. Thankfully, we'll be able to go home soon, but with that comes a great fear. A fear that she could leave me for Nate. I mean, why wouldn't she? Nate is her true love.

I knew the instant that I heard his name, my life would never be the same. I didn't need to ask why he was alive and even now don't want to know how it's possible. He's alive and that's all there is to it.

Arion hasn't said much about the situation and I don't want to pry, because honestly right now it scares the shit out of me. I can't lose her.

I know if she were to leave me again, I...I couldn't make it.

One of the nurses comes in with her chart in hand and says, "Dr. Wellington should be in shortly to evaluate her."

"Are we still going home today?" I ask.

"Hopefully." She turns away without another word.

When we got to the hospital, Arion was awake and fine. Then the doctor and nurses started to ask her what happened and she had a panic attack. They made me leave 'til they calmed her down. It was almost impossible – they ultimately had to give her a light sedative – and then a psychologist evaluated her mental state. He determined that she's on the verge of a breakdown and we have to tread very lightly with her treatment.

They started her on some anxiety medication and I know that has helped. It's the same shit I used to take to get spun out of my mind on, but taken responsibly *can* provide real help for anxiety.

Letting go of her hand, I lean back in my chair, running my hands over my face. *Please let us be able to go home today. She's not happy here.*

As I remove my hands, she's staring at me. "Hey, baby. You okay?" I ask.

"Yeah. This bed just sucks."

"I bet it's better than this chair."

She gives me a fake smile and looks away from me, like she has for the last two days. Her walls are back up and slowly she is pushing me away. Watching her stare into the corner of the room kills me. Getting up and out of the chair, I walk around the bed and get in her line of sight. She tries to move and turn away from me, but I don't let her. Moving in, I grab her face, turning it towards me and force her eyes to look into mine.

She blinks still trying to turn away from me. My heart aches by how she is acting. I just want to climb atop her and tell her how much I love her. To show her how much she means to me. Maybe that would make a difference and bring my girl back.

"Baby, please. Please don't push me away."

She releases a long exhale and looks me in the eyes. I can't help but rub my thumb over her sweet lips. "I'm not trying to, Bain, trust me."

"But you are. Arion, I love you more than anything in the world and I can't bear to see you like this. I'm here for you."

"I know you are and I appreciate that, I just don't really want to talk about things."

"I can respect that, what you're going through is unreal. But I don't want to lose you. Please don't let things change with us, regardless of what's happened. We'll figure all this shit out *together*."

Arion blinks a few times causing tears to drop out of the sides of her eyes.

What the fuck am I supposed to do?

"We'll talk when you are ready, okay?"

"Okay," she whispers.

The doctor comes in, interrupting our conversation. Quickly, I stand up, letting go of Arion's hand to shake his.

"How are you today?" I ask.

"Fine, fine. I think the better question is how is Arion?" He looks at her and she wipes the tears away. I grab her hand giving it a light squeeze to reassure her, to push through this.

"I'm okay."

"You sure?"

She nods her head and smiles at him. "Good, well, your vitals look great, stable, and the nurse tells me you haven't had any more panic attacks."

"No, I haven't, the medication has helped."

"Good, and I trust that you are going to keep meeting with Dr. Crones?"

She looks at me and I answer for her, I know that's one of the things she doesn't want to do, but at this point I would tell any lie just to get her out of here.

"Yes, she will. I have his number and will call his office as soon as we are home."

"Glad to hear. Now Arion, you remember what the triggers of a panic attack are, right?"

She nods her head and he lightly pats her shoulder. "I'll sign the release papers, there's no reason to keep you here any longer. You two take care."

"Thank you, doctor," I tell him as he exits the room. "God, I can't wait to get you home."

"Me too," she agrees.

The nurse comes in and gives us her release instructions. Then I help Arion get dressed. She seems to be a little happier now that we are going home. Typical hospital protocol is that she be wheeled out in a wheelchair. Her facial expression is priceless when the nurse tells her this and it cracks me up. I can't help but laugh at her, causing her to glare at me.

Once she is situated, we head down and then outside. I hail us a cab and the nurse helps her inside and then I follow. Once I have the door closed, I feel like I can breathe. Everything is going to be all right, it has to.

I tell the cab driver where we are headed and wrap Arion as tightly as I can in my arms, resting my chin on top of her messy blonde hair. On the drive we sit in mostly silence, both of us watching the sights of New York City pass us by, my mind racing, wondering what the future has in store for us.

It's not long 'til we're home. I pay the driver and hop out of the cab, breathing in the fresh air. Looking up at our building, I pray being here doesn't give her a setback. I worry that it could. It's the last thing I want. Over the last few days, I've witnessed it firsthand and it's horrific. Watching the person you love struggling to breathe is indescribable. The way she panicked and didn't make sense of her words was absolutely heart-wrenching.

As I open her door, she looks unsure. I decide to lift her out myself. It will be easier to be in control and quicker if I have her in my arms where she's safe. "Ready, baby?"

"Uh-huh," she responds.

I kiss those sweet lips, the ones that take my breath away as I cradle her body against my chest. For the first time in a few days, she looks me in the eyes without me having to beg or plead. Then she closes them, and I take her inside.

Herbert opens the door for us, welcoming us inside. I thank him and breeze right along to the elevators. I'm on a mission with Arion in my arms. I'm thankful that the lobby is empty. We catch the first elevator right up and my heart thuds against my chest as each floor ticks by. I'm scared that walking down the hallway will trigger another panic attack for Arion, or worse, what if Nate's in the building?

I know that's nonsense…he won't show back up here. He loves her, and he doesn't want to cause her any harm. Saying the word "love" and thinking of another man makes me feel ill. But if he does show up, I've notified security to keep an eye out for him. The elevator finally stops on our floor. I look down at Arion as she grips my chest and whisper, "I love you, baby."

Her lips pucker and she presses them against the fabric of my shirt. It feels so good, to see her kiss me like this. I walk as fast as possible. Glancing down, Arion is clinging to my body with her eyes screwed shut avoiding the hallway with everything she has. Quickly, I fish my keys out of my pocket and open the door the best I can with Arion in my arms. I just need to get us inside. I rush us in like a vortex, kicking the door closed behind me. Looking around, it pains me how normal our life was two days ago. Now nothing feels normal.

I walk us into our bedroom and notice Arion's office is still set up on our bed. Her laptop, Blackberry, calendar, iPad, everything is as it was the last time she was home.

Setting her on my side of the bed, it hurts to let her go even though it's only for a few seconds. I gather all of her belongings and place them neatly on her nightstand. Then I lift the covers and slide us both underneath.

With her warmth around me and mine around her, this solitude is perfect. Taking the covers, I pull them over our heads where we can just be...

I wake to whispers, so close, yet so far away. Pulling the covers off of my head, it's dark. The sun has set and Arion isn't next to me. Fuck, where is she?

Looking around, it's so dark I can barely see in front of me. I blink a few times, then turn my lamp on and spot her. She's on the bottom edge of the bed, sleeping and...whispering. Scooting over, I take a closer look to try to and make out what she's saying. She looks in pain, so instinctively I go to wake her. Then she says, "Bain." That one simple word leaving her lips freezes me. It stops me dead in my tracks and I forget about everything else.

I listen some more, hoping to get a glimpse into her tortured mind, but all of her words are mumbled. Nothing is clear enough for me to make out. Then she rolls over towards me, her arm goes flying and hits me in the face. I do my best to contain my laughter. *Jesus, she's so cute.*

She moves some more, clearly restless, and her clothes twist exposing one of her tits. I can't help but groan wanting to suck it.

"Harder," she mumbles tightening her thighs together.

Fuck, she's dreaming about fucking me.

Leaning down, I press my lips against the skin of her nipple, so soft and warm, 'til my mouth forms around it causing it to harden and become erect. I leave a trail of kisses all around, claiming what is mine. Yes, her nipple is mine, she is mine, and I'll be damned if I give up.

With my mouth latched on, her body bows. Her doing so makes me suck hard and I move on top of her. With my free hand, I slide it underneath her and she arches for me so I can bring our bodies close together.

She moans knotting her fingers into my hair, while I keep sucking and kissing. My cock is stiff and wants her so bad. With just our clothes separating us, I press myself against her pussy. Letting her know how much I want her.

She doesn't open her eyes, but I know she's awake. "Fuck me," she whispers. There's my girl, as eager as ever. I smile, so happy to get a piece of who she was a few days ago, even if it's only for a little bit. We've been through some shit these last few days, but I know I can make all that go away. Binding our bodies together as one does something to our minds and our souls. My lips move urgently on their own, drenching her skin, *my skin* with kiss, after kiss, after kiss, twisting and pulling her clothes every which way so I can touch every bit of her skin.

She moves her hands through my hair gripping hard and then she roams my body. Covering every part of me, 'til she reaches my pants and goes inside. The instant her soft hands form around my hard cock, I want more and begin moving my hips. Pushing and pulling, pumping myself in her grip.

Suddenly, out of nowhere, my mind begins to race to images of her leaving me for Nate. My chest tightens in pain, as my heart skips a beat. Dammit, I need to stop thinking like that. She won't leave me – she can't. "I love you, baby," I tell her.

"I love you." Hearing her say the words is just what I needed. Well, that and her pussy. Moving my hands, I pull her shorts and underwear off. She sits up and lifts her tank top over her head, leaving her perky tits staring at me.

I rip my sweats and t-shirt off in the blink of an eye, lying back down on top of her, pressing both of us hard into the mattress. My cock yearns to be inside of her and she wants it. She's so wet that the small pressure of my dick against her sex causes me to slide right in.

As I enter her body, I grunt out in pleasure. It sounds barbaric, but I can't help myself. Even though it's only been a few days, it feels like a lifetime and I don't stop moving 'til I'm all the way inside of her. Then bracing my weight above her, I claim her mouth and hold her face. Moving like I have so many times, only this time, it feels different. Like everything is fucked, but I know it's just my mind again. I move a little faster, letting the pleasure take over and push me out of this world.

With my eyes tightly shut, I focus on our release. Except mine won't come. That fucker standing in the hallway keeps creeping back up in my head. I fear this could be our last time together. She's better now…she's calm and has had time to come to terms with things. She's got the medication to help as well and…I can't keep going there. I won't go there.

My eyes fly open and Arion…my beautiful Arion brings me back to reality. She's moaning and close to letting go, I can tell by her noises. Her hand is around one of her nipples, pinching and pulling. Watching her like this puts me into my zone, exactly where I need to be.

Putting my hands into fists, I rest them at her

sides so we can come together. Nothing or no one is going to stop me or take that away from me. Leaning up, she watches me and I watch her, pumping myself with speed in and out of her delicious cunt. She tightens and squeezes me, putting my body right on the edge of explosion. Her ivory tits bounce with each thrust. Her beauty is something else.

I'm so close, but I hold back 'til she lets go, working her over and over. She throws her head back. "Yes, baby, make me come," she cries out in a fit of passion, followed by her signature orgasm sounds.

Right away, my body lets go, coming violently inside of her. I grunt like an animal slamming myself so deep. We relish in the pleasure before coming back to reality, and I take my time milking out every last drop of cum. With her eyes closed and her breathing heavy, I'm scared of what to do next. Afraid to move or speak, so I just lie down, leaving our bodies connected. My heart pounds rapidly, my head next to hers, and both of us are silent.

CHAPTER 3

-Arion-

My breaths are shallow and heavy. Everything is so different. As much as I want to pretend that it's not, it is. Everything that has happened worries me, and quite frankly I'm…scared…of the future. I'm scared of what has to be done. Clearly a decision has to be made, but how? How in the world do you choose between your past and your present? *God, please give me strength.*

Bain's body is on top of mine and his cock is still inside of me. This is my solitude, or it was. Up until Nate came back, being with Bain like this made everything better. Now as I lay here with him, I'm questioning everything. Everything that I once knew and was so sure of…is all gone. Jesus, I'd give anything to go back to how things were a few days ago, but I can't. I can't.

I waited months for Nate, practically a year,

and now that a motherfucking miracle has brought him back to me, I don't know what to do. Fear consumes me. I'm flooded by it. And the events of the other day just repeat themselves over and over in my head.

I loathe the decision ahead. It's something that I never dreamt I'd have to do and I really don't want to. I wouldn't wish it on my worst enemy, but it is there and in no way can be avoided. Since I fainted in the hallway, I've kept quiet. I know Bain wants me to tell him that everything is going to be all right, but I don't know that it is. So I can't give him false hope. It's more like I need him to tell me that.

My mind is really all over the place. Spinning, racing, vying, and I just want it all to stop. The sex helped, like it always does, but I don't want that kind of band-aid with Bain, not anymore. I don't want to use our love or what we share in the wrong way, to hide what's really going on.

Bain's breathing has changed, so I know he's asleep. Sleep might help me too. Right now, it might be my best course of action. Staying awake and battling my own mind isn't going to do anything. So I close my eyes searching for the darkness, but it doesn't come.

Nate is alive. Fuck, he's alive and I have no clue how it's possible. I know right now I can't make a decision to save my life, there is too much to process. So I fight through the ugliness that is haunting me, off to my special place, a place with Bain, a place that I always find peace in. Taking my mind back to the moment I saw him on the plane. The joy I felt running to him was indescribable and I need that again. Then I get a flash of Nate down on one knee when he proposed and I know from now on my special place will never be the same. There is adoration in Nate's eyes, as he looks up at me. I visualize it clear as day. Fuck, this is all too much to handle. I pray for answers and sleep. Thankfully it's not long before sleep takes over.

"I don't know about that, Mom. She's just…not the same. She's…she's quiet." I hear Bain in the distance. When no one responds to him, I realize he's on the phone.

I blink a few times, trying to pull my bearings together and listen. As much as I know I shouldn't, I can't help myself. It may give me a glimpse into his head and where he is mentally. As this point I need all the help that I can get to make a decision like this.

"I don't know what will help."

He exhales loudly. I can hear the sound of the coffee pot brewing in the kitchen. The sun is bright, shining in all of the windows and I wish today was supposed to be as we had planned for our weekend before the…what should I call it?…incident. No electronics or contact with anyone, just us.

"Don't you think I thought about that?" His tone is a bit agitated, then he whispers, "I'd fucking marry her if I thought it would help things."

My heart stops, shocked at his words. We've never discussed marriage, so I can't believe that is what he just said. I really shouldn't be surprised. I know that Bain and I have so many plans for the future, but marriage hasn't come up yet.

I continue to listen, even though I know it's so wrong. I just can't stop.

"That's not how she is, Mom," his voice is laced with annoyance and a hint of emotion. *He's crying.* Fuck, I have to figure out what to do. Suddenly he is very far away and I hear the click of the patio door shut. I sit up and look through the condo. His gorgeous frame is standing outside, leaning over the balcony railing. Maybe talking to him can help me decide what in the world I am supposed to do. I get up and find my clothes scattered about the room. Seeing them like this reminds me of the time we shared last night. I put them back on and head right towards Bain. We have to talk about things. I can't go on like this anymore.

Thankfully he is no longer on the phone. He's resting back on one of our lounge chairs with his arm draped over his eyes, wearing only a pair of his underwear. The second the door clicks when I close it, he sits up looking at me. It's a warm summer morning, the sun baking our patio and us. Bain wipes away his tears when he sees me and it kills me that he's so upset. He opens his arms to me. I go to him, sitting between his legs. He smells divine like always, mixing up my brain and making it hard to think.

"Did I wake you?" he asks.

"No."

"You sure?"

"Yeah," I respond, trailing my fingers over his tattooed chest, as my head rests comfortably on him.

"Are you okay today?" he asks me.

Shaking my head, I look at him and say, "I don't know, Bain. I just don't know what I am, or what to do."

"I know, baby, I feel the same way."

Looking at him for the answers, I ask, "What would you do?"

"Oh, baby, I can't answer that. I'm biased."

Clinging to him, I hold on, afraid that I'm going to lose what we have. Then the words that have been haunting me for the last three days leave my mouth of their own accord. "I'm scared."

"I know. I'm fucking petrified, baby." He strokes my hair saying, "I can't lose you, Arion. I don't want to unfairly ask you to choose me, but I cannot fucking lose you." His voice cracks and he holds me as tight as he ever has.

"I don't want that either."

Then Nate crosses my mind and my heart hurts. Nate. I have to see him. I can't avoid the situation forever. Thinking of him gives me a different feeling than what I share with Bain.

With Nate, there is a sense of security – safety. And with Bain, there is nothing but pure, raw desire and passion. I love them both but on two totally different levels. My stomach turns thinking of the differences and knowing that I have to decide.

"Arion, I know you have the world's hardest decision to make, and I don't know what's going through your mind. But I'm begging you with everything inside of me to put into consideration how good we have things. We have come so far, and our life is amazing."

"I know, Bain. Trust me, I love our life and you. But I also can't ignore the fact that Nate is alive and once upon a time he was my future, and he and I shared what you and I have."

We sit silent for a few minutes, neither of us saying anything. I know that my words hurt him, but I have to be honest with him. I'll always be honest with Bain, no matter how bad it hurts.

"I need your help deciding what to do. I have to talk to Nate, as much as I want to act like this never happened. I'm completely lost as to what to do and I know you can't tell me…but I want to make sure that you know what's going on."

"I know. I know you have to talk to him and

I don't want to be the one to tell you that you can't, because he *was* your first love and you both had planned a future together. But I truly think as long as you follow your heart with this, we *will* stay together. I'm sure you have so many unanswered questions. Like I do, so I can't tell you how to handle things. Because if I did or if I was really being honest, I would..." he trails off without finishing his sentence.

I have a pretty good idea of what he is going to say. My heart aches thinking of his earlier words. *I'd fucking marry her.* Jesus, what am I supposed to do?

"Maybe you should call Nate's mom or dad and talk to them?" Bain suggests. "They've been like parents to you."

"Yeah, that's a good idea."

"Do you wanna head in and eat breakfast? You need to take your medicine."

"Sure," I respond, completely forgetting that I now have to take something daily. I stand and he reaches for me, standing himself.

We head inside and I lie on the couch. I can tell Bain wants everything to get back to normal, but in the back of my mind, the thought of Nate is knocking and I know it won't go away 'til I see him, or better yet, make a decision of what to do. Bain comes back handing me my phone. I take it from him, not sure what to do with it.

Deep down, I love Bain so much. I really do, but I *have* to see Nate. My heart is telling me that and I'm so scared that seeing him is going to evoke all sorts of emotions and feelings inside of me. Feelings that…I'm not sure what to do with.

Unlocking my phone, there are a few texts from Aubrey, so I text her back, *Sorry, I haven't been in contact much. My mind is a mess. Could we do lunch?*

Right away she responds, *Of course. I'm just going to throw this out there though 'cause I can't imagine the shit storm going through your brain. Why don't you come stay with me for a while for a clear perspective on the situation?*

I think about her text and listen to my voicemail. There's just one and I'm shocked when I hear Jeff's voice on the other end of the line.

"Arion, Nate told me what he did. I'm sorry that Barb and I didn't tell you sooner. We had intended to, but…Barb is really sick. She's in bad shape right now, and that's part of the reason why Nate showed up at your place. He wanted you to know and we couldn't bear to tell you ourselves. Plus, I knew if you came to the house that it would spill the secret, that Nate was alive. Anyways, it's all out in the open now. We should talk, call me. I hope you're doing better."

Setting my phone down, I feel uneasy about the news. Barb is sick? What does that mean? Picking up my phone without thinking, I dial Jeff.

It rings and rings and rings. Finally, he answers. "Hey, how are you?"

"I'm okay. I got your message. How's Barb? What's going on with her?"

"She's doing the best that she can. She hasn't been feeling well for a while now and recently got worse." He catches me up on her medical situation, and I just feel awful.

"Christ, I'm so sorry. I had no idea. I should have stayed in better contact with you guys."

"Arion, it's all right, there's nothing you could have done. And with Nate being back, had you tried to stay in contact, I probably would have stayed pretty distant. Speaking of Nate, he told me what happened. How are you feeling?"

"I'm better, now that I'm home. But my mind is just a mess."

"I know, dear. I'm so sorry."

"What happened? I mean, I have to know how this is even possible, that he's alive."

Jeff sighs heavily. "He's a strong man, Arion. He has been through so much. His Humvee drove over a roadside bomb in Afghanistan. He and one other member of his platoon survived. They were taken hostage and somehow survived almost a year of torture."

Tears fill my eyes, thinking of Nate being held hostage. I can only imagine the horror that he endured.

"Arion, I know you've made a new life for yourself, but you're all that kept Nate alive while he was gone. He's really having a hard time since coming home and not having you in his life."

"Jeff." My voice cracks as I say his name. "I never planned for any of this to happen. I thought he was gone, like we all did. For Pete's sake, we buried him."

"I know, dear, and Nate knows that too, but it wasn't his time. I can tell you that he loves you more than anything in the world."

"I know. I…" I trail off without finishing my sentence. I can't bring myself to say the words, but the truth is that I never stopped loving Nate and I don't know if I ever will.

"He wants to see you. He meant no harm when he came to your place. He's in bad shape and is healing the best he can. He lost part of his leg when he was gone and mentally he's pretty messed up."

"I know he didn't mean for anything bad to happen, it just caught me off guard. He was the last person I ever imagined to see."

"Arion, I know you need some time to figure everything out, but please know that both Barb and I are here for you if you need anything at all."

"Thank you, Jeff. I really don't know what to do. I just need some space to sort things out. Please tell him that, but I'll be in touch.

"Okay, I will."

"Oh, how's Zeus?"

"He's good. He's such a happy pup now that Nate is home. I know it was hard for you to leave him with us, but it all worked out with Nate coming back."

"Thank you for taking care of him."

"Of course, dear. You take care of yourself."

"You too."

He hangs up and Bain walks over to me with

a huge cup of coffee in hand. "Was that Nate's dad?"

"Yeah, he left me a voicemail and said Barb is really sick, so I called him back." I take a sip of my coffee then settle into the couch.

"What did he say?" he asks.

"That Barb is sick and that's partly why Nate came here."

"Do you believe that?"

"I don't know what to believe, Bain, everything is such a blur."

"I know, baby," he says pulling me close to him.

"He also said Nate was held hostage for almost a year and lost part of his leg."

Bain reaches over and rubs my back. "I'm sorry, Arion."

"This can't really be happening, can it?" Tears well in my eyes and he takes my coffee from me, setting it down and then scoots closer, wrapping me in his hold.

"Don't get upset, baby, we'll figure this out…together. You hear me?"

Nodding my head, I hold on to Bain with everything I have.

Together…together…together. The word rings in my head. If only it were that simple.

CHAPTER 4

-Nate-

"Seriously, Dad, you have to let me call her. I'm losing my mind over here…I need to talk to her."

"Nate, I won't do that to her and you shouldn't either. You need to show patience and let her be, dammit. The poor girl has been through enough already. Do you really think it's a good idea, when she asked for space?"

I shake my head knowing he's right. The last time that I saw her, I put her in the hospital. The last thing that I want to do is cause any more harm. When she's ready she'll come to me. I need to give her time. It pisses me off that I have to, but I do.

"I got to get to a meeting, son."

I nod my head, doing my best to stay calm; I have to keep my temper under control. It's my own fault I can't contact her right now. I made the decision to show up at her house and now I have to pay the price.

He gives me a hug and says, "Thank you for taking care of your mom today."

I watch him leave, resting my hand on top of Zeus' head, taking a few minutes to myself. Fuck, I just want to see her. But then I get a flashback of her collapsing in the hallway and it reminds me why I have to wait 'til she's ready.

I take a few deep breaths and head down the hall to my mom's bedroom. She is lying comfortably on her bed, with her Kindle in hand, reading being one of the last pleasures left to her.

"Hey, baby," she says.

"Hey, Ma." I set my crutches propped up on her dresser and lie on her bed; Zeus lies next to it on the floor. Since I've been home, he has been by my side non-stop. "How are you feeling?" I ask.

"I'm okay, how about you?"

"I don't know, Mom."

"Wanna talk about things?" she asks.

I can't help but chuckle at this. That's all I feel like I do anymore, from one doctor to the next. But I know she's only trying to help. "What is there to talk about? Arion's with someone else, and she wants nothing to do with me."

"Oh, honey, you don't know that."

"But I do, Mom. I can't even see or talk to her. I tried and we both know what happened."

"I know it seems like there is no hope for you two, but just give it a little more time."

Looking at my mom, I hide my true emotions. Inside I go from rage, to pain, to glum. She might think there is hope, but I on the other hand, do not. "I've given it time. Waiting around is killing me."

"I know, dear, and I'm sorry. Let her process things and I'm sure she'll come to her senses."

"I'm glad you're optimistic, 'cause I'm losing hope."

"You can't lose hope Nate, never no matter what. You hear me?"

Nodding my head, I roll to my side. "You're her soul mate and that is something that Bain can't change. Don't give up on her."

"I won't. I couldn't imagine living forever without her. I just want what we had before I left."

"You will, dear. Remember hope, never let go of it."

In a way my mom's words soothe me. She has a way of calming me. I just pray that she is right. My biggest fear would be living this life, in my condition, without Arion. I push that all aside, not letting those negative thoughts creep in any more. Keeping myself calm, my eyelids feel heavy and I let them close. Thinking back to the last time she was in my arms...

Goddamn myself for making this decision. Staring at Arion's tear-stained face, I hold it tightly in the palms of my hands. "I'll be back, A, no matter what. You hear me?"

She nods her head sniffing, trying to stop herself from crying.

"I love you so much. Hold on to that and know that I'm always thinking about you. You're always in my heart," I manage to tell her.

"I love you," she whispers.

"I love you too. Remember, I'm doing this for us. To give us a better life."

"I know," she responds and nods her head. But does she? Does she really know why I'm doing this and just how much she means to me? Checking the clock, I know I don't have long. I have to go. I hug my parents, both with smiles as big as the sun. They are staying strong for me. My dad did this years ago, so he knows how hard it is to

say goodbye before being deployed.

Leaning down, I give her one last kiss holding her chin with my thumb and forefinger. "I love you, Arion LaSalle, and I promise I'll marry you the day I get home."

She smirks and nods her head. "Love you too," she whispers. So small and fragile, her usual confidence stripped from within. With those sweet words from my one and only, I turn and leave my family. But I have faith in God that I'll be back. I know now is not my time, he won't do that do me.

"She knows that, Nate," my dad says sitting on the edge of my bed. "She knows you never intentionally meant to upset her, this is just a lot for her to handle. She cried herself to sleep for the better part of a year when she thought you were dead. Then when she finally moved on, when she finally got a new life and her shit together, it all came crashing down."

"But it doesn't need to. She can come back to me, we can figure everything out. And Bain...well, I'm sure he has hundreds of women throwing themselves at him."

"Nate, it's not that simple. I've seen them together; I don't think it matters who is throwing themselves at him, he wouldn't look in their direction. He actually reminds me of you, and how you and Arion used to be."

"What the fuck, Dad, whose side are you on?"

"Yours. Always. But I'm going to be honest with you about all of this—it's not as easy as Arion letting him down gently then she comes running to you. There's more to all of this. And for now, you need to give her a little space, let her wrap her head around everything. She'll come around and you'll get your time with her, I can promise you that."

"I just don't get it...why isn't she ready to see me now?"

"I think she's scared."

"Scared of what?"

"If I had to guess, I would say her feelings and what that means for her, or maybe another breakdown."

My dad's words make sense. I know I'll get my time with her, but waiting is going to be absolutely excruciating.

"Listen, you get some rest, son. It's been a long day."

I give my dad a hug and sit alone on the edge of my desolate bed. Then as I look into my closet, the glint of metal of my dumbbells catches my eye. I'm not even sure I can lift them, but I need to start making a change. Leaning over, I pick them up and figure I'll at least try. Surprisingly, they aren't too heavy. I get situated, holding both of them while balancing my elbows on my knees and begin to pump my arms. Right away, everything inside of them burns, but it feels so good to be doing this.

I know I'm not the man I was when I left, but I can get back to him, minus my leg of course. Minor point. I continue to go 'til I can't anymore and drop my dumbbells on the floor. Looking down at my scrawny arms, I know it's going to be a lot of work to get back in the shape I was in.

Rolling over, I grab my laptop and turn it on, heading for my latest obsession: Arion's Facebook page. It's the closest thing I have to being involved in her life. I'm not sure if she knows that we are still friends, but we are. I've searched and been through everything possible on here, but maybe today there will be an update, something that will give me a hint as to what she's thinking. Unfortunately there are no new posts like I'm so used to seeing. So, I click on her photos and scroll through to find my favorite one of her. She's looking through a window. The reflection of her is gorgeous, so perfect and pure. The glass almost makes her look angelic.

Staring at it, I pray that she will come back to me. I mean, really, how can she not? She's just scared and I'm sure trying to figure out how to let Bain down. That has to be what's going through her mind. Plus she knows that we belong together. Even though it pains me, she can take all the time she needs.

CHAPTER 5

-Bain-

"Please, James, just get me one more day. Just one more day."

He grumbles into the phone. "Jesus Christ, one more day, Bain, but that's it. Don't ask me again. I won't let you jeopardize your career before it even starts."

"Thank you, I promise I won't."

I hang up and go in search of Arion. She is right where I left her. Stark naked and gorgeous, soaking in our oversized bathtub.

"Hey," I say as I begin to undress, she looks at me with an eyebrow cocked and then scoots forward so I can slide into the scalding hot water behind her.

"God, I love holding you in my arms," I whisper behind her ear and lean us back together. She sighs heavily as do I, and then there it is, the awkward silence. I don't know if it's her or me, but it's there and it scares the shit out of me.

"I talked to James," I tell her, trying to spark up conversation.

"Yeah?"

"Yeah, he said he'd get me out of practice again tomorrow."

"No! I don't want you to miss practice again. Not because of me."

"I'd rather be here with you 'til I know you're ready to move past all of this."

"I'm ready."

"You are?" I ask confused.

"I mean, I don't know. I'm ready to focus on work, but I can't decide what to do. I just don't know, Bain."

"Baby, I don't want to be the one to force you to do this, but in order for us to move on, you need to talk to him. You can't act like he's not back and everything is as it was before, because it's not."

"I know, trust me, I know!" she snaps in frustration.

I stay quiet not wanting to upset her further, or push the subject. Deep down, I don't want her to see Nate again or to talk to him for that matter. I could only imagine how he's going to act to try and win her back. But in my heart, I know this is what's right.

"You could invite him over here?"

She looks at me with a blank expression and doesn't respond.

"You'll be most comfortable in our home. He can come when I'm here and I'll give you privacy. But most importantly, I'll make sure that you're okay."

Hearing myself invite him to our home is a bit crazy, but I care for her enough that her safety and happiness mean that much to me.

"I don't know. Can't I just keep acting like that part of my life is all a dream?"

"You can't, baby. Put yourself in his shoes."

"It's just…" She trails off and stares away from me.

"What, love?"

"I'm scared at what seeing him will do to me. What feelings it will evoke and most importantly, how it will affect us."

Hearing her say that takes my breath away. So this is why she's being so resistant. She's scared that seeing him will be the end for us. I search for the right words to say, something that can comfort her in this moment. But I've got nothing. There is nothing that I can say or do, because the truth is that true love prevails. The question is, whose love is stronger? Anger fills me. I couldn't imagine my life without her. I'd lose my goddamn mind and I don't want that, that's for fucking sure.

"I'm sorry," she responds.

"Don't be," I say, holding her body tightly against mine. If my time with her is limited, I have to make the best of what time we have. "I love you, Arion, more than anything or anyone in the world, and I can't imagine the predicament that you're in. For that, I'm sorry. As much as I want to make you choose me…I can't, but I can show you how much you mean to me, how much I love you, and how my body yearns for you like nothing else."

Reaching around her, I slide my hand down her soft body, adoring every curve that she possesses. She leans her head back, letting all of her weight fall against me. Her arms drip water, and I finally make it to my heaven – her sweet cunt. Even though we are submerged in water, she's still wet. I move my fingers inside of her soft folds and over her clit. She moans a little and turns her head into my neck. Leaning down, I search for her lips. Letting her know what I want, she parts them slightly, breathing softly and looks at me.

I watch her while I sink two fingers high inside of her. As we kiss, I'm scared – scared that this is going to be the end for us, but I push away those thoughts and do what I promised myself I would do a long time ago. I focus on making her happy. It's all that I can control in this moment.

My body aches for more, I need to be inside of her. But first, I please her, rubbing vigorously back and forth over her clit, while my fingers feel her. She begins to moan, really giving in to what I'm doing, so I don't waste a second taking her out of this world. My hard cock throbs against her back and I sit us up a little. I know making her come will clear her mind; it's what she's always turned to for relief.

I work her clit like I have so many times. Just the right amount of pressure to get her there, she writhes on top of me. And I count down waiting for her screams. She holds on to her orgasm as long as she can, she says it makes them that much better. Three, two, one…it's easy, like clockwork, baby.

Her entire body arches out of the water, her hands search for the tub, gripping the sides, trying to give herself some friction to hold on to.

"Yes, baby. Let go," I tell her. "Come for me."

Her noises increase as she enjoys the pleasure, then suddenly she quiets down and her body stops shaking. We both are breathing heavily and I bring us back under the water, sliding myself inside of her, instantly I fit right in.

"Oh God," she says, leaning into my neck, and I begin moving, pushing and pulling inside of her. Her cunt is so tight and mixed with the water makes the friction unbelievable. My insides crave her; even when we fuck, it's not enough. I continue to move, over and over, and work her 'til she begins to give in, moaning louder and louder. Ever so slightly, she moves her body along with mine and begins matching my thrusts.

My body wants to come. I've always said my dick has a mind of its own, but I fight the feeling, knowing that I won't let go, not yet anyways. Then all of a sudden, Arion sits up and takes control, moving along my shaft. My eyes go right to her ass, then my cock, as our bodies mold together.

Taking my hands, I hold her ass and help guide her. She tips her head back, her long blonde strands dipping into the water and then she lets go. I follow suit, slamming her hard on my cock. My body quakes from head to toe and I'm forced to close my eyes, although I don't want to take them off of her. She slows, as do I, and her beautiful body lies back on top of me.

"Thank you," I tell her. Surprised that she took the lead.

"You don't need to thank me. Thank you for everything."

Then she stands and holds her hand out to me. Reaching up, I grab her hand and stand, both of us never taking our eyes off of each other. As I step out of the tub, she hands me a towel and we begin to dry off.

"Do you have practice the day after tomorrow?" she asks me.

"Yeah."

She doesn't say anything else and my mind starts to wander. Maybe when I am at practice she will go and see Nate? I don't really believe she would go behind my back. I have to trust her and at the same time, I have to support her. If she sees him, so be it. I need this over with just as much as she does. God won't take her away from me. I know he won't... *he can't*.

"Bain, if I invited Nate to our home, could I talk to him alone, maybe when you are at practice?"

"I'd rather you not. Why does it matter if I'm here anyways?"

"I just don't know how I'm going to feel, or what I'm going to say, and I...I need to be able to speak openly to him."

"I understand and you can do that with me here. Baby, I don't want him upsetting you and something happening without me somewhere close. He can barely help himself, much less you, if something were to happen to you again."

"Come on, Bain, that's not fair to say. He's been through a lot and when he was here last time, I was caught off guard. He shocked the shit out of me."

"What if he does that again? What if he proposes or something crazy to try and win you back?" I ask, aggravated that she is defending him, though I know what she says is true.

"Bain, he won't. Trust me. I know Nate, better than anyone does. I hate to say it, but he already proposed. I guarantee that he just wants what is best for me."

"Please, baby, we don't know how you're going to react. He'll never know that I'm here. I just need to be close in case I need to help you."

"No, Bain, I'll be fine. I just need to talk to him alone."

"Arion, I obviously can't stop you, but I really don't think it's a good idea."

"Really, I'll be fine," she snaps.

I nod my head in disappointment and get dressed. Then we head into the living room, mixed emotions running through me. I'll be damned if I let this ruin my day. "I'm sorry, I got frustrated, babe. I'm just…" I trail off. How the fuck should I say what's on my mind without sounding like a complete jealous ass. "I'm scared."

"Scared?" she questions me, hopping up on the cool granite of our countertop, sitting in her normal spot. "Well, I'm scared too."

The worst part about me telling her how I really feel is that she doesn't tell me that everything is going to be okay and there is nothing to be scared about. She just agrees with me.

Jesus, if I could just get into her head for a

few minutes, then I feel like things would be better. Even if I don't agree with what she's thinking, it would at least answer some of my questions. But where I stand now, that's all out there with no definitive direction on how our lives are going to be, or where things are headed. Knowing that yet again, this argument is a lost cause, I change the subject. "Are you hungry?" I ask.

"No, not really."

"Come on, babe, you've barely eaten any-thing lately. I'm sure something sounds good."

"I don't know, maybe the Metro Café?"

"That's perfect, let's go out and get you something."

"Okay," she says and I step to her. She won't make eye contact with me and I'm getting tired of things being like this with us. Holding my ground, I place my hands on her sides and watch her intently. She doesn't last long and finally looks at me. I smile and lean in, kissing her gently. She kisses me back the way she always has, strong and with confidence. My hands find her head, cupping it and holding us together. Threading my fingers into her soft blonde strands. As we kiss, her phone rings in the distance. But I push away the anxiety. I know that everything is going to be all right – it has to. Pulling away, I help her off the counter.

"Shall we?" I ask.

"Yes."

We slide on some flip-flops and leave hand in hand. She doesn't slow or falter in the hallway, like I'd worried. This is the first time we've left since we came home. I'd been anxious about how she would handle stepping foot in the spot that her breakdown happened, but it's like nothing to her. I seem to be more stressed about it. On the elevator ride down, she hugs me and I tightly hold her back, resting my chin atop her hair.

The lobby is quiet. Herbert is off today and for once I'm kind of thankful. With all of the stress flowing through me, I'm not in the mood to talk. Once we emerge into the noisy busyness of New York City, the sun is warm and I go to hail us a cab.

"Let's walk," she says, stopping me by grabbing my arm.

She never wants to walk, as it always seems that I get recognized, so I'm a little thrown off by her request. "You sure?" I ask.

She nods her head, wrapping her hand tightly around mine and we head off. I love how confident she is leaving the house at the drop of a hat, with no make-up on, messy hair, and whatever clothes she threw on.

Internally, I again want to bring up the fact that I don't want her to see Nate alone, but how can I? I know it will ruin our lunch. "I'm surprised no one is recognizing you," she says.

"Right? It feels good," I respond, as we round the corner on our last leg to the Café.

"Bain, I want you to know that no matter what happens, I love you, okay?"

"I know, babe, and I love you. Can I ask you a question?" She nods her head looking up at me with those gorgeous light eyes. "Are you doubting us? I mean, are you having second thoughts that we are going to stay together?"

"No! I mean, I don't know. I just…I just want you to know that I really and truly *love* you."

"I know that and I can't imagine my life without you, I love you just as much. I know what we're facing is difficult, but can you promise me one thing?"

"Of course."

"If you talk to Nate, will you please talk

things over with me afterwards? I mean, you owe me at least that much, right?"

"Of course I will."

She nods her head and I stop us right in the middle of the sidewalk. There are people bustling by, but I don't notice any of them except for her. She's all I ever see. Taking her head in my hands, I thread my fingers into her hair. Her eyes look at me searchingly, and I claim her mouth. Wrapping my lips around hers, tight and hard. I kiss her with all of my might. My tongue barges access to her mouth and she accepts me, wrapping her arms around me.

As I stand here and kiss her, showing not only her, but the world that she is mine, tears fill my eyes, tears of fear and worry. She is truly my everything, and without her…I am nothing.

CHAPTER 6

-Arion-

Standing on the side of this busy New York street with Bain, we embrace and kiss. I feel a passion inside of me that only he makes me feel. But still nagging at the back of my head is Nate – my Nate. He is alive and back. It's something I only dreamt of, but now it's true. I give Bain everything that I am, knowing what I must do.

Thinking about my plan makes my insides heat with anxiety, I'm not sure how he is going to handle things, but I know in order to work through all of this, I have to take a break. Once he pulls away, his face is red and cheeks are tear stained. I hate that a simple kiss can do this, but right now it can.

Bain smiles at me and we continue to walk. My appetite is no longer there. Well, truth be told, it hasn't been there at all lately. I begin to replay in my mind what I'm going to say, but it all jumbles together and I know I'm just going to say how I feel and wing it, hoping for the best.

When we enter the Metro, it's slow, and both of us take a moment to look over the menu. I try to decide on something that will be light on my stomach and order a bowl of soup. Bain orders a pasta bowl, then we both sit down to wait for our food. He hasn't said much since our kiss and neither have I. I can sense his eyes all over me. The same way they were the night that we first met. But that night, I was free. Yeah, I was in pain, but I didn't have the weight of another pulling me towards them. Though it had been difficult to decide between holding on to the pain of losing Nate or letting go of it to allow myself to move on. If only I'd known then, what I know now.

"Arion?"

"Yeah," I respond.

"I can't take the silence, baby. Please, say something, anything. I need to know what you're thinking."

With one heavy exhale, I look him right in the eye. "I'm going to stay with Aubrey 'til I can figure out what I want. I need a clear perspective on things and—"

He cuts me off, "No, no, no, no, no. Please, baby, no. Anything but that. I'll leave our house if you need the space, but not her house."

"Why?" I ask confused.

"Because it's minutes from his and I'm too far away if something should happen to you."

"Oh, Bain, I appreciate you worrying, but Aubrey has next week off of work, so she'll be there with me. I really need to just clear my mind. I can't do that at our house."

"So you already talked to her about this?"

I nod my head, clearly seeing that he is getting frustrated.

"Arion, please, baby. I'm begging you, I can't..." He puts his head in his hands and it kills me to see him like this. Tears stream down my face watching my actions cause him this much distress.

"I'm sorry," I whisper.

"Me too, Arion. Me too."

The server brings our food over and sets it in front of us. Bain looks at it with as much enthusiasm as I do.

"I can't eat," he says.

"Me neither."

Finally he looks up at me. He's so broken. Maybe I shouldn't leave. Maybe I should just stay at our house. I break our gaze, not able to look into his eyes anymore.

"Are you ready?" he asks me.

I nod my head and go to stand. He holds his hand out to me, and I grab it. I'm still unsure how we ended up in this situation. It was never my intention to hurt him, but that is exactly what's happening.

On the walk home, neither of us speaks. We just take our time, with the occasional photo and shouts at Bain. Walking at this slower pace, Bain lowers the brim of his hat. I know he's not in the mood to deal with fans right now. My mind races a million miles a minute and I wish that I could turn it off, to just enjoy this time with Bain. As I look over at him, in a pair of basketball shorts and a t-shirt, he is the sexiest man alive.

I used to think that about Nate, but things are so different now. As I weigh the pros and cons of both guys, it's just too much to handle and I know that I need to go to Aubrey's. As much as I wish I could stay at our place in the city, I just can't.

I need clarity, another person's perspective. I

know Aubrey can give me that and she invited me to come and stay with her. She is my best friend after all.

As we walk into the condo, I feel sick that I'm about to leave not only Bain, but our home. I wish it wasn't this way, but my heart is telling me that this is what needs to be done and I have to follow that. Bain flops down on the couch, throwing his arm over his eyes. I grab my phone and text Aubrey. *I told Bain. I'm gonna pack some stuff and head your way.*

I'm here, doll. Call me on the drive if you want.

Before I just go and pack my shit, I sit down on the couch next to Bain's feet. He lifts his arm and looks at me, then covers his eyes again.

"Trust me, baby, if I thought there was any other way I could make this decision, then I would. But I really need some time away to just focus on what's best to do right now."

"Arion, I'm sorry, but I don't agree with you leaving me. I think it's absolute bullshit."

"I'm sorry, Bain, please know that." I stand and walk to our room, tears streaming down my face. As quick as I can, I grab my backpack and shove as many clothes in it as will fit. Then I collect my purse, putting my iPad and phone in it.

I take my things and set them by the front door and go back to Bain. He's still in the same spot. This time I kneel on the floor next to him and pull his arm off of his eyes. He's a mess, but so am I.

"I love you," I tell him.

"I love you too," he responds. "How long are you going to be gone for?"

I shake my head, not able to give him an answer.

He frowns, shaking his head back at me and I kiss his lips. The second our mouths connect, it is pure passion. Everything inside of me burns and I know that I have to stop it. But Bain takes his hands, grabbing the back of my hair and weaves them in, holding me close. I love the way he controls me and he knows that. I can tell what he is trying to do.

He's hoping that he can distract me, which normally would work, but right now I have to be strong for myself. In order for me to decide what to do, I have to leave.

Even though it weighs so heavily on my heart and hurts to the point where I just want to give up, I can't. I can't because I know both Bain and

Nate are depending on me.

As I pull away from Bain, he sits up not wanting to let me go. But I break our kiss and tell him, "Goodbye."

He sits there shaking his head, and with all of my will and my strength, I move forward. My heart burns and my throat feels like it's going to completely close at any moment. It reminds me of my medication, which I grab from the kitchen counter and drop into my purse. I can't bring myself to look back at Bain; instead I grab my car keys and open the door. Quietly, I pull it closed behind me, and the second it's shut, my body wants to collapse on the floor, just like I did the day Nate was standing in the hallway.

But I will myself forward, my strength persevering. On the elevator ride down, I open my bottle of pills, taking one for my anxiety, hoping it will bring me back to reality and restore some normalcy with my breathing.

"Oh my God, I'm so glad you're here," Aubrey tells me as she embraces me in a huge hug.

"Thank you for letting me stay with you."

We separate and I set my bags on the floor.

"How are you holding up? You don't look so hot."

"I'm not. This is all just a fucking nightmare."

"I'm sorry. I can't even imagine what you are dealing with." I take a deep breath letting her words sink into my head. Neither could I, until now. Aubrey heads into the kitchen and asks me, "Do you want a beer?"

"Yeah."

As I sit on her couch, I'm taken back to the day that I made the decision to leave New Jersey. I never thought when Bain and I drove away to embark on our future that something like this would happen. God, everything feels like it has washed away, and now here I am in the clusterfuck that is my life.

"Here, sweetie," Aubrey says handing me my drink. Without even thinking, I take a long sip, allowing the alcohol to burn on its way down.

"So what's going through your mind?" she asks me.

"Everything," I quip back, barely able to keep myself from crying.

"Be a little more specific please."

"Aubrey, what the fuck do you want me to say?"

"How about where does your head stand right now?"

"I'm at a loss, very confused, and scared. I know I need to see Nate, and last time that didn't go well. But I have to do it. Then when I do, what do I say? On the other hand, I have Bain at home, hurting in the most unimaginable way, because I left him."

"A, I really think at this time you need to only think about yourself. I know that sounds selfish, but if they keep burdening you, trying to make you choose, it's not gonna help you make the right choice. You need to make a decision based on yourself, okay?"

I nod my head, hearing what she is saying. I know that is what I have to do now; just doing it is a whole different thing.

"Clearly, you still have feelings for Nate, or you wouldn't have left Bain."

"I love him. Dammit, Aubrey, I love them both."

"I know, sweetie."

"Let's talk about Nate. Besides the incident at

your house, have you talked to him?"

"No, not at all."

"Do you want to?" she asks.

I think about her question for a moment, then answer. "I do."

"So, I think you need to get that handled first. I hate to say that Bain will be waiting for you, but he will."

I take another sip of my beer and sink down into the couch.

"What if I don't feel anything for Nate anymore?"

"Then you go back to Bain."

"But what if I feel what I had with Nate, like he'd never left?"

"Then you have a tough decision to make, but I really don't think that you will. I think your heart will pull you towards one or the other."

She's probably right. "I'm sorry to come barge into your house like this with all of this drama about me. I should have asked, how you're doing?"

"I'm fine. And you don't need to be sorry at all. This is what friends do."

She wraps her arm around me and we sit in silence, sipping our beers. Then my phone chimes in the distance and I get up to check it. "Are you hungry?" she asks.

"Not really, but I haven't eaten much for days, so I probably should."

"I think I have an old, frozen pizza in here from ages ago I can heat up." I can't help but laugh.

"Sounds good."

My phone shows a missed text from Bain. *Fuck, I miss you. I love you so much, baby.*

Before I respond, I think about his text and how to write him back.

"Who was it?" Aubrey asks.

"Bain." I pass her my phone and say, "I don't know how to respond."

"A, the best advice that I can give you is to be honest with both of them, always, throughout all of this. What does your heart tell you to say?"

"I love and miss him."

"So text that back and let it go for now. I think you have a bigger obstacle ahead of you with seeing Nate. What are you going to say to him and how can you be sure that you don't have another panic attack and end up in the hospital?"

"You sound just like Bain. Like I told him, Nate caught me off guard. This time, I'll be prepared to see him."

CHAPTER 7

-Nate-

How the fuck did this happen? How the fuck did this happen? As I sit on the floor of the living room completely shaken up and bloody, my body is unsure. One minute everything was fine, then the next, one of my worst nightmares came true.

"Why don't you shower, sweetheart?" my mom asks me.

I shake my head looking up at her. Again feeling like a failure of a person.

My dad finally walks back inside. Pain is written all over his face. He looks just as upset as I am. "How are you, son?" he asks kneeling next to me and rests his hand on my back.

I shake my head, not able to answer him.

"You did everything you could."

"No, I didn't. If I had both legs, I could have run to him faster."

"I'm sorry, son. I hate to ask, but the vet wants to know if you want his ashes back."

"Fuck!" I shout, knowing that we are going to have to break the news to Arion that Zeus died. I can't imagine hurting her again, I just can't.

"Should I call Arion?" my mom asks.

I hate to cop out, but I sure as hell don't want to be the one that has to tell her. "I guess. She needs to know and she's probably not ready to hear it from me."

My mom kisses me on the forehead and then walks off to make the phone call. "I really wish he'd shower," she tells my dad on her way to the kitchen.

Glancing down, my pants and shirt are covered with blood. So I listen to my mom, willing myself to get up and into my bathroom. After I peel my clothes off, I throw them in the trash and get into the shower. The hot water cascades over my body and as I sit there, I break down.

I'm such a fucking loser. I mean, I couldn't even save my own dog from dying. Anger and pain wash down the drain with the light pink remnants of the last of his blood. I can picture him in my arms, after my pathetic ass finally made it to him.

I punch myself in the fucking jaw in anger and grab the bar of soap, washing myself as fast as I can. Then trying not to think, I get up, soaking wet and balancing on my one leg. I grab a towel and wrap it around my waist. Leaving my crutches behind, I hop to my bed. I just want to sleep so I can wake up and this will all be a dream. But as I cross the floor, my foot slips from the water and I have nothing to hold on to. I fall hard, smack in the middle of the bathroom. My body lands like a ton of bricks.

What else could go wrong today? I take a deep breath and force myself to get back up. I grab my crutches and stand on the rug for support. I dry myself off and then leave the bathroom. This is the exact reason I need to start building my strength. Clearly I can't help myself. It's been shown more than once today. After I dress, I lay down on my bed, doing my best to clear the pictures of Zeus from my mind. I even will my brain back to Afghanistan in hopes that the pain of being there will wash away the events of today.

As I wrestle in my own mind, something in the distance pulls me towards it. My ears open as wide as they can. Listening to the voices outside of my room, I swear I hear Arion, but I know it's not possible. Then clear as day, I hear her say, "What happened?"

Fuck, she's here. She's at my house. *But, how did she get here from the city so quickly?* I force myself up and pull a hoody on to hide the scars that cover my body. Then with all of my might, I go to her.

The second I open my door, I can see her. She's sitting on the living room floor, with Zeus' blue ball in her hand – crying. The tears stream down her face and it kills me to know that yet again I am responsible for hurting her. Watching her so perfect and beautiful with her long, blonde hair all over to one shoulder, I can't move. She doesn't see me and quite frankly maybe it's better that way. Both of my parents are talking to her, trying to calm her, telling her that it was an accident.

I know as much as I want to avoid telling her what happened, I have to. As quietly as I can, I move towards her. My dad sees me coming and nods his head, like he is proud of me. I get close enough to sit in front of her, not scared of her reaction this time. If she came here, she obviously is ready to see me. On the way down, I grab my dad's arm.

As my body descends she looks up at me, not paying attention to anything else except looking deep into my eyes. I smile and once I am at her level, I scoot a little closer, so I can touch and comfort her. She sobs harder, throwing her arms around my neck grabbing my sweatshirt. This is the moment I've dreamt of, for damn near close to a year. I never imagined that our dog dying would be what brought us together, but sadly it is.

She nuzzles into me, the way she always did, and I do the same. Breathing in her sweet scent, the scent of paradise. And for the first time in almost a year, my body awakens, everything inside of me feels alive, including my dick. *Fuck, she still has that control over me.* I pray that it won't get too hard. The last thing I want to do is freak her out, but fuck, I've missed her so much.

"I'm so sorry, A," I whisper, not able to control my lips as they kiss her neck. "I'm sorry for everything." Sorry for leaving, for showing up at her place the way that I did, and for letting Zeus die.

She breaks down crying even harder and I

just hold her. Wishing that even though we are hurting, this moment would never end. I finally have her in my arms and I don't want that to ever change. My mom rubs my head and I look back to see my parents walking away. *Alone at last.*

Arion looks at them as well and then rests her forehead against mine. As we sit together like this, I can almost taste her. However, my mind and body are on two different axes, both wanting something totally different. My body wants her so bad. From my hands, to my mouth, to my cock, every bit of me wants to claim her. But my mind is telling me that one wrong move could ruin everything. It could cause her to have another breakdown, or freak out and leave.

Finally she pulls her head up, her plump lips parted and tear-stained cheeks all yank on my heartstrings.

"I don't even know where to start," she says and pulls away from me.

"Please don't do that. Please, A, just stay where you are."

She comes back to me, my dick now so hard that I have to put one hand in my lap to cover it.

"You can ask me anything."

"What happened to our baby?" she asks in a broken tone and begins to cry again.

I tilt my head back and exhale heavily. Then I cup her cheek, to get her to look at me and to my surprise she leans into my touch. "I took him to the dog park, like I have so many other times. You know how good he is, I normally don't even take a leash. I park close enough and he just runs to the gate to go in. It's been a way for both of us to get out of the house." Suddenly, the events all replay in a flash and I have to stop talking. How do I tell her? "I parked and let him out of the car, then before I knew it, he ran off after a squirrel and across the intersection. I tried to get to him, A, I really did, but with my leg and my crutches, I couldn't. It all happened so fast. By the time, I had him in my arms, he took a few breaths and—"

I can't finish the sentence. My throat closes telling her that I'm the reason our dog is dead. Because of me. Both of us break down crying again and in that moment, all we have is each other. I cling to her like my next breath and she does the same.

I'm not sure how long we sit like this, tears rolling and our bodies just together. After a while, both of us are quiet and I fear what will come next. So I continue the conversation, in hopes that if I keep talking she will stay. I never want her to leave.

"I'm sorry about Zeus. And the other day, too. It was way out of line for me to catch you off guard like that at your home. I don't know what I was thinking, I was just going mad without you."

She gives me a small smile. "It's okay, Nate. The more I thought about it, I'd probably have done the same thing. Except had it been me, I would have come to see you the second I was back in the States. Why did you wait?"

"My parents told me that you had moved on and I wanted to respect that. At one point I'd planned on possibly never telling you. But then when I came home and I didn't have you, I started to lose my mind. You are all that I think about, and finally one day, I just called a cab and the rest is history."

"Oh Nate," she says and puts her head in her hands. I stroke her blonde hair and hope I'm not upsetting her any further. "As much as it hurts being pulled in two different directions, I'm glad to know you're alive. I wouldn't have wanted to go through life with you alive and me never knowing."

Her words give me hope. Hope that she is here to mend our relationship so we can move on to the future – together. Jesus, I'd love nothing more.

"Then, I'm glad I told you."

"I'm sorry that I didn't take Zeus to the city with me," she says.

"Don't be. I'm glad I got some time with him when I got home."

CHAPTER 8

-Bain-

I can't believe she's gone. She's really fucking gone. My biggest fear in life is living without her and right now that is exactly what I'm fucking doing.

I knock back another glass of Highland Park. It's so smooth, but still not enough to take me to the level I need to relieve this pain. There are only two things in the entire world that can do that, Arion and...pills. I know I swore when I stopped taking pills that I'd never start again, but I also stopped because of Arion and now she's gone.

I can't get ahold of her, she's not texting me back like normal, and I just don't know what to do. I could pay someone to kill Nate, that's what I could do. Without him in my life, fucking everything up, things would be exactly as they should be. I know it's just the Highland talking though. This was Arion's favorite, we bought it when we moved into our condo to celebrate and she loved it so much that she wanted to savor every glass. Now here I sit, drinking it all alone.

My phone rings again, and of course, it's not Arion. I ignore James knowing he will leave a voicemail. Fuck, he's so much to handle right now. I listen to it curious about what he wants.

"Glad to hear you went to practice today. I heard you came down pretty hard on your knee again. I hope it's doing okay."

As I set my phone down and take the last drink of my ten thousand dollar bottle of Scotch, something clicks. I know that I shouldn't do this, but I have to find some relief somehow. I function well on pills and if the team prescribes them to me, then I can't get in trouble for taking them.

I grab my phone and scroll through the contacts 'til I land on the team physician's number. It might be a long shot, but what the hell. I clear my throat while it rings, hoping I sound sober enough to talk to him.

"Hello," he answers.

"Hey Lawrence, it's Bain Adams."

"Hey Bain, how are you, man? Is your knee doing okay?"

"Actually that's why I called…it's not feeling great. I've been icing it since I got home today, but it's been killing me. The ice has kept the swelling down, but Jesus, it's sore."

"I was worried about that. Do you want to swing by my office before I leave and I'll check it out? I can do a quick x-ray and maybe I could give you something for the pain."

"Yeah, I think that would be best."

He gives me the address to his office, then we hang up.

I hop up thankful that my knee doesn't really hurt. I head into the bathroom and look into the mirror, studying my own reflection as it stares back at me. Fuck, I look buzzed, so I turn on the shower and hop in right when it's cold, hoping the jolt will sober me up. Damn, it burns, but at this point, I'd give anything to feel something other than my own heart being torn from my chest.

My body is shivering and I'm wide awake. As I turn the water off and get out, I envision Arion is in front of me. I can see her soaking in our large tub, so comfortable and relaxed and beautiful. I know with shit like this happening, I need these fucking pills.

I finish getting ready and then head downstairs, hailing a cab to Lawrence's office. I rub my knee as the driver weaves in and out of the crowded New York streets. I hope this will make it red so it doesn't completely look like I am lying. Even though I totally am.

His office is just a few blocks from the condo, I could have walked, but considering my fake injury, I chose not to. Plus, I'm not 100% steady on my feet at the moment.

After I pay the driver and crane my neck looking up the length of his tall office building, I take a mental note to never buy another bottle of Highland Park. *Pull your shit together*. It's a quick elevator ride up to the 17th floor and as soon as the doors open, I spot his office.

Walking in, the décor is modern and there is no one behind the receptionist's desk. Then Lawrence rounds the corner.

"Hey, how are you feeling?" he asks me.

"I'm good, just having some pain in there," I respond following him back to an exam room.

"Let's get an x-ray first," he tells me. Right away I fear the worst. I know it's not gonna show anything. But I'm here, so I let him do his thing.

"Thanks for seeing me on such short notice," I tell him.

"It's not a problem, I do what I can for my players. Let's go in here," he says after we are all done with the x-ray.

I sit on the exam table while he pulls the image up on his laptop. "Has it been bugging you before today?" I shake my head and then the image appears.

"Here we go. See here?" he says pointing at the screen. "You have an awful lot of scar tissue. That may explain why your knee may bother you and swell up at times, and it probably always will. But thankfully, nothing is torn or broken. I think you just tweaked it pretty good. I'm gonna give you a prescription for some Percocet. I think a few days of rest and by Monday, you should be good to return slowly. How does that sound?"

"It sounds great, Doc." I keep my words short, in hopes that he doesn't catch on to that fact that I am drunk.

"Good," he says and signs a prescription. "Call me any time day or night if anything should worsen, okay?"

"Thank you." I slowly get off of the table,

making sure on my way out to limp.

As I head back down, I feel guilty. This is the same feeling I got when I first started to take pills. But deep down I know the benefits that they provide me. They did back when I lost Kinsey, and I know they'll help now.

I wake to the sound of my phone ringing. My face is pressed into the carpet. I'm sprawled out, half-dressed, and can barely remember what I did last night. Maybe it was the alcohol. Fuck, no, it was the pills. Dammit, I cannot believe that I gave in the way that I did. My phone rings again. Maybe it's Arion calling, so I will myself to get up, but then it stops and I let my body collapse against the floor.

As I glance around the house, everything is a mess. There are things broken and I know I got out of control last night. Then I turn my head to the right and next to me is a picture of Arion. It's my favorite. She's absolutely breathtaking in it. I took it when we were on vacation. She's staring through a window, light eyes, messy hair, and nothing but love shines from her. That was when everything was different. Now, here I lay with nothing but a fucking picture to console me. Christ, my life is wrecked without her.

My body is so jacked up from sleeping on the floor. I don't care what happens, I'm never taking pills again. I get up and my phone rings again. I spot it right away on the bed and pray that it is her. My heart is telling me that it is. I answer right away.

"Baby?"

"Bain?" My mother's tone is broken, she almost sounds like she's been drinking.

"Mom, is everything okay?"

"No, baby, it's not. It's really not."

"What's the matter? Why have you been calling me over and over?"

"I only called you once."

She sniffles and I ask again, "What's the matter, Mom?"

"That asshole took a plea deal."

"What? For how long?"

"Not long enough, something crazy like twelve to twenty years."

"Fuck," I snap and sink to my knees, my back leaning against the frame of our bed. "That fucking asshole fucking killed her."

"I know," she says crying. "It's not long enough."

"Mom, it doesn't matter what they sentenced him to, it'd never be long enough. Does Dad know?"

"No, I have to call him now."

"Do you want me to come down there?"

"No, you stay home and take care of yourself and Arion. I'm gonna call your dad. If you talk to the DA, will you please let me know if she says anything new."

"I will, Mom."

We hang up and my mom's words replay in my mind, *Take care of Arion.* I can't do that if she isn't here, but I couldn't tell my mom. I check the call log and notice she is the one who called. Right away I dial her back. My body courses with anxiety. I've been waiting for what feels like forever to talk to her.

"Hey," she answers in a quiet tone.

I almost cry at the sound of her voice. "Hey," I respond back, trying to keep myself calm.

"How are you?" she asks me.

"Baby, I can't answer that. I need you here."

"I'm sorry, Bain."

"Me too," I whisper.

"Are you coming home soon?"

"I don't know what I'm going to do. I know I woke up missing you and needed to hear your voice."

"God, I miss you. You have no idea how brutal it is without you. You should come home. Please."

She's quiet for a moment, then says, "I need to make my mind up first."

"What's to figure out?"

"Come on, Bain, don't be a dick."

"It's a legit question."

"I need to sort everything out in my head. I've only seen Nate once."

That's why she wanted to go to Aubrey's, so that she could be close to him. Fuck, I'm slowly losing her. She is slipping from my grasp.

"Are you there?" she asks.

"I'm here. I'm just a little shocked that you are hanging out with him, that's all."

"It's not like that, our dog died, so I had to go over there."

"Oh…I'm sorry, baby. Listen I'm probably not the best person to be talking to right now. I'm not myself when I'm not with you and I got some really shitty news about the trial just now, then you tell me that you are hanging out with Nate. It's all a lot to handle. Arion, please remember what you promised me."

"Of course. Bain, I'm sorry."

"Me too," I tell her and hang up angrily, cutting her off as she begins to speak again.

I know deep down that this isn't the way that I should be acting, but I don't give a fuck at this point. She won't come home.

I look out into the rest of the house and spot the bottle of pills that Lawrence gave me. I know I said I wouldn't do it just minutes ago, but I also never expected hearing that the asshole who took Kinsey's life would be getting a fucking measly twelve years in jail then out walking the earth. Then Arion tells me that she's seen Nate and isn't coming straight home and it's all too much to handle. I open the bottle of pills and pour them into my hand, counting how many I have left. Damn, I took twice as many as I should have last night. No wonder I crashed on the carpet.

I decide on popping a few right now. I'm actually excited for the high that I'm about to receive. That's the beauty of pills. They give you something to look forward to. Even in the depths of despair, the darkest of all days, one tiny white pill can shine light on you like the sun does from up above.

I begin with two pills and head to the couch. Soon, that's not enough and I take another two. Letting the sensation of my euphoric high take over. If I close my eyes for long enough, I can feel Arion on top of me. This is right where I want to be, with her, always and forever.

CHAPTER 9

-Arion-

With my head in my hands, I just don't know what to do. I've been up for half of the night trying to decide between Bain and Nate. The problem is that both of them are so amazing and I love them both so much that the decision is agonizing.

Aubrey finally wakes up, walking into the living room with a messy mound of her brown hair piled on top of her head. "Morning," she says.

"Hi." I roll over and pull my feet up so she can sit next to my feet.

"How did you sleep?"

I can't help but laugh. "I didn't."

"Damn, I'm sorry, girl. Did you talk to Bain?"

"Yeah. Finally, this morning he called."

"And?"

"He's not good, at all."

"I can imagine. I hate to say it, but you really need to make a decision. I mean, what's the point of waiting any longer?"

"I know I need to, but saying it and doing it are two totally different things."

"I know. Let's talk about things."

"I really don't think I want to right now," I tell her being completely honest. I'm tired from not sleeping and am not sure my brain can function enough to make such a life affecting decision.

"Well, tough shit, you need to. You're the one that has to make this decision, no one else. You can't leave these two hanging like you have. Especially if Bain isn't doing well."

I tilt my head back and stare at the ceiling, thinking of her question. My heart aches for both Nate and Bain, and I know as much as I keep making excuses for not deciding, I need to. Being in Nate's arms was so comforting, it was everything I used to have with him. From the way he held me, to how he looked in my eyes.

But then there is Bain and the fire he puts inside of me is something on an entire different level. I melt at the pure sight of him and that's not to mention what his touch does to me.

"So what does your gut tell you right off the bat?" she asks me.

"I love them both, I really do. But I love them in different ways. I waited for Nate for almost a year and during that time I ached for him. Every ounce of who I was needed him. He never came back to me. Then Bain emerged into my life and I fought my feelings for him with all of my might. But everything about Bain is powerful, and I failed, succumbing to him and everything that he is."

"I don't think you can ever love two people the same. Even parents, they love their children differently. I mean, look at me and my sister, for instance. Polar opposites."

"The problem is, I do love them both."

"Who do you see your future with?"

"I had everything planned out with Nate. He asked me to marry him, we talked about kids and how we wanted to grow old together. With Bain, I don't know what he wants. We haven't talked about those sort of things."

"Arion, does any of that really matter, or is this about taking each day as they come and being happy while you do it? What's meant to be will be. I mean, who cares what you've talked about, because God can rip it all away at any moment and there is nothing you can do."

"You're right. This is about whom I whole-heartedly love. Regardless of the past, or the future. I think I know what I need to do."

"Good, you know I support you regardless of your decision."

"I know. Would you mind if I had Nate come over here? So we could have some privacy? I'm sure his mom is home and I want to talk to him without anyone lurking."

"Of course you can. I'm actually headed to the gym."

Aubrey walks off and I dial Nate's house number. It rings a few times, then he answers. "Hey, how are you?" I ask him.

"I'm better now. Is this for real, are you really calling here?"

"Oh stop it, Nate. Listen, I need to see you, can you come over to Aubrey's?"

"Of course I can. Is everything okay?"

"Yeah, it is."

We hang up and I give Aubrey a hug on her way out. She asks what my decision is. I knew it would be too long for her to wait without knowing who I've chosen. She looks at me with genuine happiness in her eyes and says, "Stay strong, A."

"I will."

I know it won't take Nate long to get here, so I do the best that I can and pull myself together. Then as I finish brushing my teeth, I hear a knock on the door. Right away, my stomach goes into my throat.

I head towards it and as I stare at the white paint, I exhale and pray what I am doing is right. Nate knocks again, clearly impatient. I open it and look into his eyes.

So bright and clear, messy hair and rough face, even skinny, he can take my breath away. He really is beautiful and will make someone happy, unfortunately I love Bain so much and because of that, it won't be me. I hold back the tears, knowing what I have to do, and put on a fake smile for him. *You can do this, A.*

"Hi," he says, with a smile and sparkling eyes.

"Hi," I say, barely choking out the word. I welcome him in and then hug him, wondering if one more embrace will help anything at all. Maybe it will change my feelings? But as he gently holds me back, I know we can both tell it's not the same as it used to be.

I guess it's because we're both so different now. He smells like Nate, a scent I dreamed about for a long time, but even smelling that scent again doesn't compare to the ravishing yearning I have inside of me for Bain. He does something different to me. I wish I would have seen that sooner and wouldn't have run away like I did.

"Come in," I tell him stepping out of the way. I feel bad seeing the back of him and how you can tell that part of his leg is missing. As I close the door and turn to him, I lead us to the couch. "Let's sit," I tell him.

"How are you?" he asks, following me.

We both sit down and look at one another; it is so strange to be staring at him again. A million different emotions flow through me and I can't help but cry. I'm not sure if I *can* let him go. After all of the nights I cried myself to sleep praying for a miracle, and here he is. Wiping the tears away with the backs of my hands, I look at him. He has his hands in his lap and is just watching me, I can see there is a glimmer of hope that exudes from within him and he finally says, "Come here." Opening his arms to me, I scoot over, not able to fight his request and let myself indulge in Nate one last time. Yeah, it might seem selfish, but it's what I feel I need to do. The second he embraces me, I cling to him, holding him tightly back. He soothes me by rubbing my back.

"I don't even know what to say," I tell him, afraid to start the conversation and let him down.

"You don't need to say anything, A. That's the beauty of our relationship. I am perfectly content just having you in my arms." His assumption that we still have a relationship catches me off guard. Maybe it's because I called him over here, but whatever it is, I am not sure I like it. He knows that I am with Bain.

I slightly pull away, feeling guilty for being so close to him. "Are you okay?" he asks. "You seem different than the other day."

"I'm fine, Nate, I really am. I'm worried about Bain, that's all."

"Did something happen?"

"Not really, he just didn't sound like himself when we talked this morning."

"I'm sure he's not. He's gotta feel a lot like I do."

"Which is?"

"Lost. Alone. Sad."

I look away from him, hating knowing that my actions are responsible for doing this to not one, but two people. "Don't beat yourself up, A. It's not your fault that you're so amazing and we both love you."

"I'm not beating myself up," I snap, angry that he can read me so well.

"I know you, Arion. I know you almost better than anyone. You can't lie to me."

In my mind, Bain consumes me. He is all that I'm thinking about and it is clouding my thoughts, making me know what I have to do.

"I'm sorry, Nate."

"Sorry for what? You haven't done anything wrong."

"I'm sorry that I wasn't there for you and that I haven't been."

"It's fine, A, things happen. It was crazy of me to think someone as amazing as you would have stuck around and waited for me."

"I did, Nate. I waited for months and months. Bain and I were just friends and then it turned into more. I didn't plan on this happening."

"I know you didn't. It's just a lot to deal with. Coming home and not having your partner and then finding out she's moved on with some millionaire basketball star."

I don't even know where to go with this conversation. Do I sit here and try to justify my relationship with Bain or who he really is? I don't want to share anything personal about him, to say that we connected over our grief, with the death of his sister and me thinking Nate was gone, but we did. And Bain is so much more than the fame that shines down on him.

"I don't know what to say, Nate," is all that I get out.

"Come on, A, I know you better than that. Just talk to me."

"Nate, if you want me to be honest with you, Bain consumes every part of my life. I'm sorry."

Nate surprises me; my comment doesn't seem to hurt him at all. He looks at me and says, "Don't be sorry. Talk about Bain. Arion, I've had a lot of time to think about things. I'd be lying if I told you in the back of my mind I wasn't surprised that you moved on. Still it doesn't make it any easier, but it's the truth and that's all I want between us – the truth."

Hearing him say that's all he wants from me pushes me to do what I know I have to. My heart is with Bain, it has been since the moment I laid eyes on him and acted like he did nothing to me. My future is with Bain as well. Yeah, it might be a little more uncertain than what Nate and I had planned, but it's what I want. "If you want me to be honest with you, my heart is with Bain."

He leans back and looks at my expression, like I am joking. "Arion, please. Please don't do this."

"Nate, I'm sorry, trust me," I say doing my best to hold back the tears. "I'm not saying I don't love you, because I do and some part of me always will. But what I have with Bain is different, the hold he has over me is something I've never known."

"I can give you that too. I can give you anything you want. You said it yourself that you still love me. Let's at least give this a try."

Taking my hands, I remove his from around me and look him straight in the eyes. "I'm sorry, Nate, so sorry."

He places his hands on his thighs and looks up to the ceiling, exhaling.

"Is it because of my leg?"

"What? No, come on, you know me better than that. My heart wants what it wants. I'll always be here for you, if you ever need anything. I know you have a tough road ahead of you."

He laughs sarcastically and looks at me, "Yeah, okay, A. I need all of you. Not just you as my friend. Don't you see that?"

Tears roll down my cheeks, looking him in the eye. I never dreamt of this in a million years. What I pictured was God giving him back to me and us riding off into the sunset together. Now here I sit, a monster. Only a horrible person would do such a thing, wouldn't they?

"Isn't there anything I can do?" he asks.

As much as I wish there was, there isn't. Painfully, I shake my head at him, tears running down my face. He grabs his crutches getting off of the couch.

"I don't want to say this, but...clearly, I don't have a place in your life anymore, and with how badly my heart and body ache for you, we can't be friends, A."

I stand and hug him one last time, knowing now that this is really goodbye. Even though this is what I want, I can't stop the tears as they stream down my cheeks. I try to calm myself hoping being in his arms again will…but it doesn't.

Nate cries too as he holds on to me and it kills me to see him so upset, especially after what he has been through. It's the last thing that I want.

With my heart making my decisions today, I know what I did was right. I need Bain, he would make everything better right now. Damn myself for leaving him. Pulling away from Nate, he looks into my eyes and nods his head, then turns his back on me. The second our flesh disconnects, it's as if that's the true end for us. In this instant, everything that we were, we are no longer.

Although, I've lived this last year wanting nothing more than to have one more moment with him, he's not who I'm meant to be with. Bain is.

"Arion, I'll always love you. Please remember that." I nod my head, watching him walk away. How does someone hurt another person of this caliber? He reaches for the door handle and I open my mouth to speak. He shakes his head. "It's okay, A. You don't need to say anything. I'm really not in any shape to take care of you the way Bain can anyway. Be with him, be happy, and as long as he is good to you...that's what matters. Goodbye, Arion."

I sit stunned, barely able to comprehend the compassion that he has shown me. How? Why? I really can't understand it. He went from arguing with me that we could make this work one second to telling me that he can't take care of me the next. If it were me, and Bain was leaving me, I would fight to the death. As the front door closes behind him, I feel like I can finally breathe.

Right away I call Bain, but it goes straight to voicemail. I'm sure he's at practice. I shoot him a text instead, so excited to get back home to New York. *Baby, I made my decision. Please call me, I can't wait to be in your arms. I love you.*

Traffic was a bitch, but when is it not? As I put the car in park, I really can't fathom why I ever left here. I could have done all of the thinking I needed to just like Bain had asked of me right here. Checking the clock, Bain should be home from practice any time. It's Friday and they always have short days. I call him again in hopes that he is driving home, but still no answer.

Getting out of the car, I grab my backpack, rushing as fast as I can to the elevator and up to our floor. My stomach is a mix of butterflies and emotion. I can't wait to see Bain. God, I can't wait. As I exit the chilly elevator, and walk down the hallway, I see our door and practically want to run to it. Jesus, it feels so good to be home.

My key fits right in and I head inside, hopeful that Bain might already home. The second I step inside, I freeze. The door shuts behind me and I'm not sure if I want to go any further. *What the fuck happened?*

The house is trashed. I can't even put into words the picture before me. Everything is everywhere. It looks like the place has been ransacked. But as I start to put the pieces together, I know that's not the case. Bain's clothes are on the floor, along with a picture of me. There are other broken pictures and decorations, and on the coffee table is an empty bottle of our Highland Park whiskey, and when I see what is next to it I want to collapse. A pill bottle.

Dropping to my knees, I grab it. The label says Percocet – quantity 30. I open it and glance inside, there are far from 30 pills in here. I check the date and see it is from yesterday, so I count how many are left and know right away when there are eleven that Bain has fallen off the wagon. *Fuck, this is all my fault!*

I search the house looking for him, worried that he is passed out somewhere from so much alcohol and the pills, but only find his cell phone lying on our bed. I can tell it hasn't been slept in since I made it.

I'm starting to panic surrounded by all of this craziness. The room begins to spin and I know I have to stop the panic attack before it starts. I drop to my knees right where I am and put my head between my legs, breathing as many deep and heavy breaths as I can manage.

Don't pass out. Don't pass out. Then I force myself to crawl to my backpack to retrieve my pills. It will calm me right down and let me focus on what the fuck to do. I swallow the pill and sit, focusing on not fainting. Everything is going to be all right.

Thinking about what to do, I decide to call James. If anyone has tabs on Bain, it's him. I dial him and sit with my back against the wall.

CHAPTER 10

-Nate-

Walking away from Arion has to be the hardest thing I've ever done. I've done it once and I promised myself if given another opportunity, I'd *never* do it again. But this is what she wants and I cannot fight that. Listening to her talk about Bain and how happy she is, plus feeling how disconnected she was in my arms today was all of the reassurance I needed to know that for now I have to let her go. Even though I don't want to, I have to.

In life, one of the cruelest lessons you learn is that sometimes the right decision is the hardest one to make. Sitting in the car with my dad as we head to one of my appointments, both of us are silent. What can I say? He knows me well enough to tell by the look on my face that I just need some space right now.

In all honesty, I'd be lying if I said that this is something that I didn't expect. Because I did, from the moment in Germany when she didn't arrive with my parents. But like I said to her, I'm in no shape to take care of her or anyone else for that matter. I'm fucked up, not only physically, but also mentally.

"You know, maybe therapy today will help," my dad says.

Seriously? "Dad, come on. You know nothing is going to help."

"I'm sorry."

"Are you? You haven't even asked me what happened."

He takes his eyes off the road to briefly stare at me. "I just know you, and you don't like talking about your feelings."

"I don't, but holding it all in isn't helping."

"You can always talk to me, you know that. Are you hanging in there?"

"No," I respond shaking my head, barely able to hold back the tears.

"I'm sorry, Nate."

"I guess it is what it is. Her heart is with Bain and I saw that, so I had to let her go."

"What?" he asks.

"I can't be the man she needs right now. She knows I love her and I always will. I'll always be waiting with open arms if things change."

"Jesus, Nate, I'm shocked, I can't believe you didn't fight for her and you just agreed to let her go."

"I did, don't get me wrong. I tried to convince her, but when I saw how adamant she was, I knew it was an uphill battle. Dad, the look of relief on her face when I left made me know I made the right decision. So for a while, let's *not* talk about Arion."

"If that's what you prefer, of course. But I have to be honest with you, I still think that you're going to look back on this after some time and regret not fighting for her. The other day, when you had her in your arms, that is the happiest that I have seen you in years."

"I know and I'll always hold on to these last few days. Maybe I will regret things later, but for now I did what I felt was right *for her.*"

My dad doesn't say another word on the drive, the only sound between us is the road beneath the tires of his car. My insides are a knotted ball of pain and regret. I don't know why it's hit me so hard and so fast, but it has. I felt fine for a little while, but now with my dad's words I feel regret creeping in the worst way and I just want to make it stop. Leaning my head back I take slow, deep breaths needing to put myself into a calm state.

This is the same thing I did while I was held hostage. At times I wanted to lose my mind, but I knew that wouldn't help anything. Especially because once my captors left me, I was alone, I couldn't see, and moving only made things worse.

After breathing for what feels like an hour, nothing has changed except for my anxiety spiking. Checking the clock it's been about three minutes. Inside, the regret eats me up, and I begin to think maybe my dad was right. I probably should have fought for her; I should have tried to convince her even more that our love was stronger than anything Bain could give her. But I remind myself that this is what is best for her and her happiness. It doesn't matter how I feel inside. Arion is all that matters.

CHAPTER 11

-Bain-

...

CHAPTER 12

-*Arion*-

"I don't know, James, it's not like him to not have his phone on him. Have you talked to him at all today?" I leave out the fact of the pills and alcohol and that the house is destroyed.

"No, I haven't. Not since last night."

"Jesus, I'm so worried something is wrong with him."

"Arion, don't get yourself upset. I'm sure he just ran out."

"You're right. I'll let you know as soon as he's home." *He's fine. I know he is, he has to be.*

I hang up with James and feel a bit lost not to have Bain here. As much as I tell myself that he is okay, my insides are telling me otherwise. I grab his phone to see if there are any clues in his texts that will help me figure out where he is.

Looking through the text messages, they are

all his normal contacts. I go into a few of the recent ones to see if anything there will point me to what he could be doing…and nothing. Then I look at the call log. It's all from James and me and one that he made to Lawrence. Who is Lawrence? I rack my brain, then it clicks. I walk across the plush carpet and pick up the pill bottle. Lawrence Jenkins. The team physician. He called him last night. That must have been how he got the fucking pills.

I sit on the couch completely frustrated and decide maybe Herbert knows where he is. I head down to the lobby and am grateful that he is working today. He sees me right away and smiles like always. I do my best to put on a fake smile and not show him the anxiety that's running through my body. I don't want to alert Herbert to my mounting panic, but if Bain has left the building, he will know.

"Hi, Miss Arion, how are you?"

"I'm okay, thanks. How are you?"

"Very well, thank you. I haven't seen you lately, everything been okay?"

Crap. "Yeah, it has been. I had to head down to New Jersey for a few days, but I just got home. I'm actually looking for Bain, have you seen him?"

"Not today, but I just started my shift about twenty minutes ago."

"Okay, thank you."

"Of course. Is everything okay?"

"Oh yeah. Things are fine, I just came home to surprise him and he left his phone in the condo, so I was wondering if you'd seen him. I'm sure he'll be home soon."

My phone rings and I look at the screen. It's Jack, Bain's dad, and I answer right away.

"Hey, Jack," I do my best to stay calm and head back up to the condo for some privacy.

"Arion, it's Bain."

"What's the matter?" My heart drops.

"He's been in an accident."

Hearing him say the word "accident" knocks the air out of my lungs. "Oh God, what's happened?" I ask breathlessly, feeling all of my control slip right out of my grasp.

"I don't know the details myself. The hospital just called and asked us to get there immediately. Renee and I are on our way to Lenox Hill. I think you can get there before us if you grab a quick cab. Can you do that?"

I can barely get the words out as I grab my

wallet, my heart pounding against the walls of my chest. "I'm on my way there now," I respond and run out of the condo. I contemplate taking the stairs, right now it seems like the fastest route, but I know it's really not. Instead, I press the elevator call button and wait. Finally it arrives and I pray to God that it doesn't stop on the way down. I get lucky and make it to the lobby with record speed. As the doors barely open, I squeeze through them and sprint out onto the crowded New York sidewalk searching for a cab.

The moment I spot one, I hail it. I dig into my wallet and search for a hundred dollar bill as I slide into the back seat. All the while, my heart is still racing.

"Here's a hundred dollars. Can you please drive as fast as possible to Lenox Hill?"

I stare at the driver in the reflection of the rear view mirror. He is an older man, graying hair, and dark eyes. He snatches the money from me without saying another word and hits the gas pedal. The acceleration launches me back against my seat.

On the drive, I can't imagine what happened to Bain. An accident? What in the world could have happened to put him in the hospital? Did someone hurt him, but how, or why? *Oh my fucking god.* My breathing is starting to increase and I worry that the reason he is in the hospital is somehow because of me. I should have never left him or our home. Although I tried to stay in contact, I could tell that the separation was a lot on him.

Tears stream down my cheeks and I know a full-blown panic attack is creeping in, but I can't let it take me over, not with Bain on the line. Regardless of what or how or why he's in the hospital, he is going to need me, so I have to be strong for him.

I can't believe that after all we have been through and I finally know that I want to be with him more than anything, this is happening. Sitting in the back of the cab watching the streets of New York fly by me, this drive feels like it's taking forever. When in actuality it only takes the driver a few minutes 'til he pulls in front of the hospital.

Just as fast as I entered the cab, I fling open my door and run through the double doors of the Emergency Room. Inside it's crammed with people. Looking around, I try and spot someone with authority. Finally, I do and remember to keep my composure, wiping the tears away from under my eyes. A dark-haired woman passes me a clipboard and says, "Fill this out and wait your turn."

"What?" I snap back. "No, my boyfriend, he was brought here."

She looks at me and shakes her head in clear frustration. My insides heat with anger. What the fuck is her problem? If she doesn't like helping people why in God's name is she working at a hospital? "What's his name?" she asks without looking at me.

"Bain Adams," I respond in a quieter tone hoping that no one heard me.

She types on her computer, then says, "I need to see your ID, to give you a visitor's pass." Quickly, I yank it out of my wallet and hand it to her. I can't help but glare at her as she slowly moves her fingers over the keys of the keyboard. Finally, she prints me a sticker and hands it back to me with my ID.

"He's in room 210, but you need to check in with the triage nurse. I'll open those doors over there for you. It's straight down the hall."

I nod my head once and jog to the doors, waiting in front of them. Once they open, I'm off and down the hall. Screw checking in with anyone else, I need to get to Bain. My eyes scan the room numbers. These are in the high 100's then the hallway ends and I come to the nurses' station. No one looks at me and I scan the room numbers again, 204, 206, 208, then 210. My stomach drops. I rush in, pulling the curtain back, but it's empty. *What the fuck?* No, this has to be a fucking mistake.

Where is he? *Where the fuck is he?* Why isn't he here? My mind spirals, a million different scenarios taking place all too fast. My breathing quickens, bringing me to my knees. I place my face in my hands and fear the worst. *This cannot be happening.*

My body feels out of itself. It's just like the day I found out about Nate, when the military told us he'd died. I remind myself to stay positive. She wouldn't have given me a room number if something had happened to him. With everything I have, I lift my lifeless self off of the floor – I need to stay positive for Bain. My head spins as I stand on my own two feet, but I maintain my balance while focusing. *I'm here for Bain, I'm here for Bain, I'm here for Bain,* I repeat over and over to myself.

I head back to where I guess I should have started, the nurses' station. Looking around, this place is slammed. It's busy with nurses moving all around and every room that has the curtain open is occupied. I round the corner looking for anyone to help. Behind the counter is a shorter nurse, studying the screen of a computer. "Excuse me?" I ask, my voice is broken and I clear my throat.

"How can I help you?" she automatically responds without even looking at me.

"I'm trying to locate Bain Adams." She looks at me right away and then back at the computer.

"Are you related?"

"Yes, I'm his girlfriend."

"I'm sorry, I'm not his nurse. All I know is he's in surgery. Sit tight in the waiting room." She points to a light blue room with a flat screen TV and chairs lining the walls. "His doctor will be in soon, to talk to you."

"Surgery?" I blurt out.

She nods her head and walks off. I stand at the counter stunned for God only knows how long. My world hangs in the balance of this hospital. *Surgery* is the only word that my mind focuses on.

"Arion?" Jack calls my name and I turn to see him and Renee running towards me.

The tears that are streaming down my face run that much faster and I collapse into the arms of Bain's parents. Both Jack and Renee can tell that something is terribly wrong. As I cling to them, I fear the worst. My world shakes. I'm terrified at the thought that Bain could be taken from me. I thought losing Nate was hard, but Bain…he is my everything, he is the air I breathe, the light that I see. He's my solace in this fucked up world that I cannot bear alone.

"What happened?" his dad asks, slightly pulling away to look at me.

I shake my head, "I don't know. All I've been told is he's in surgery."

Renee sobs and I try to maintain myself when I hear a doctor in the waiting room say, "Adams!"

We all look in his direction and basically bolt across the room towards him needing answers.

CHAPTER 13

-Nate-

"I really don't understand the fucking point," I snap at my psychologist as he studies me above a thin wire-rimmed pair of glasses that sit on the bridge of his nose.

"Maybe it will help? That's all I'm saying."

I chuckle under my breath, tired of his games and sit up. "Look at me – I have one fucking leg, I barely weigh over a hundred and thirty pounds, and I just lost the love of my life. Nothing is going to help me, you understand?"

He writes something down and then looks at me. "What?" I ask. "What are you always writing down about me?"

"Notes, for your treatment. Nathaniel, I'm concerned for you. You're extremely angry, it's not like you."

"Well, like I just fucking said, look at me – I

lost Arion and I'm a bit of a fucking mess," I grit.

"I am looking at you and you look just fine to me. You need to learn to adapt to things now. Nothing is going to change going forward if you continue to act like this."

I shake my head, pissed that he isn't understanding where I am coming from. I'm tired of being the reserved guy. I'm tired of keeping quiet. No more. I've told him time and time again that since my reason for existence is gone, I'm angry. Hell, I'm more than angry. I'm fed up with the world. I mean, how can I not be? I love her and there is nothing that I could've done to change things. When you love someone the way I love Arion, it's what you do. It's what's right.

"Shall we at least try and finish today's session?"

Looking at the door, I'm really contemplating leaving. But how will that help me? I'm here for a reason. Not only does the military want me to be, but I told my parents I would keep trying.

Lying back down on the couch, I close my eyes.

"I want you to focus on going back to a memory with Arion. Preferably, when you first fell in love, but anything will do."

I close my eyes and there she is – again. Her gorgeous face haunts me day and night. Long, blonde hair, clear skin, light eyes, and those lips. So plump that my cock twitches thinking about them. Seeing her so pure and beautiful absolutely kills me and the fact that I cannot be with her, well, that is where my anger is coming from.

"Where are you, Nate?" Roger asks me.

"With Arion."

"Where?"

"It's dark."

"Look around, what do you see."

"Stars and waves. The ocean, we're at the ocean and...it's night."

"Good. What are you two doing?"

"Running and laughing, and we...we...keep looking back."

As I run along with Arion, everything is as it was before I left. I know I never should have left. All though joining the military was to give us a better, more stable future, it didn't do that. It was ultimately the end for us and almost the end for me.

"Suddenly we stop. In front of us are tons of different sand castles, all lit up."

"What is she saying?" Roger asks.

"I...I can't make it out."

"Talk to her, Nate. This is where I need you to break through!"

"I'm trying, it's like she can't hear me."

I sit down on the sand and Arion follows, sitting on my lap.

"Louder, Nathaniel."

I ignore Roger and focus on listening, trying to be part of the conversation.

"Come on, Nate," Roger orders.

I try with all of my might, but quickly I am getting pulled away. Then before my eyes, I watch myself morph into Bain and I hear him loud and clear. *Arion, will you marry me?*

"No," I yell and jump between the two of them, except when I move, my leg is gone and I collapse hitting the sand.

Looking up with pain in my eyes, I watch Anion nod her head and then throw herself around him. *Yes!* she repeats over and over, kissing him.

Sitting on the cold, wet sand, I watch how happy the two of them are and fade away, like a ghost that was never there. Opening my eyes, the beautiful scenery of the ocean and the night is gone, replaced before my eyes is the blank white ceiling of Roger's office.

I knew this is what would happen. Roger wanted me to break things off with Arion. He thought it would subconsciously disconnect me from her, but I disagreed because I knew in my gut this is what would happen. This is how things are always going to be. She is my one and only. She always has been and she always will be.

"That's all the time we have for today," Roger says. In my opinion it's another hour wasted of my life. "I'd like to see you before your next scheduled appointment," Roger says as I collect my crutches.

"Don't you think this was enough?"

"I do, but you're close to a breakthrough and I'd like to talk about it. Would you schedule something with Melinda on your way out?"

I nod my head and leave. Even though it sucks coming here, at least I have something to look forward, a reason to wake up and leave the house.

Melinda is smiling at me as I walk up to her.

"I need to schedule with Roger before my next appointment."

"How does Thursday at ten work?"

"That's fine," I tell her, knowing I don't have

a doctor's appointment or anything else going on. "Have a wonderful day, Nathaniel," she says, handing me a card with my appointment information on it.

Taking the elevator down, the same numbness sticks around. It's been there since I last saw Arion. A sickening, empty, feeling of...nothingness. I wish I had her to turn to right now. She's all I've ever depended on. On the drive home, I think back to how good things were before I ever left. Going back to that time on the beach with her and seeing her face reminded me of how things used to be. I know I will never have what I had with Arion with anyone else. But maybe there is a chance that her feelings will change and maybe we could come back together. You never know what the future holds and believe me, that's all I want. Right now, I know her heart is with Bain. It's not with me and I might have to learn to accept that. But nothing is set in stone.

CHAPTER 14

-Bain-

"Is this normal?" Arion asks.

"It can be, yes, and considering how much blood he lost during surgery, I'm not surprised. Just give his body a little more time. He'll come around." I'm groggy. Everything is foggy and my entire body hurts. The man's voice I don't recognize, but Arion's I know loud and clear. *Wait, surgery…what's going on?* I realize that I can't open my eyes. I can't see anything. Darkness surrounds me and then I try to move, but nothing happens.

Fuck! This is the scariest feeling ever. "Talk to him. Remember how important that is to bringing him out of this."

"I have been, for days, and nothing's happened," Arion says.

She has? What? I don't remember any of it.

What in the hell happened to me? I fight with all of my might, to give her some sort of a sign that I am here and I can hear her. Trying to force myself awake while jogging my memory at the same time…then it hits me. She's here. She is here with me and I don't hear Nate's voice.

"Thank you, doctor," she says. I can feel her hand wrapped around mine; it is as tight as I've ever felt.

There is silence between us, but it doesn't last long, small sobs reel out of her. Although she is trying to keep quiet, I can hear her clear as a bell. Dammit, why can't I move? Then I feel something heavy on my stomach and I realize that it's her head. She cries on top of me and it pains me to the point of breaking. Why can I feel and hear her, but I can't do anything?

Frustrated, I am lost and confused at what's going on. Then all at once it happens. My eyes open, and before me is a bright ceiling, lights shining down on us. The brightness hurts and it forces me to close them. I slowly move my stiff neck to my left, and try again. There is a machine, with cords and lines feeding in and out of it, and then I look down. There she is, *my* Arion.

"Please come back to me, Bain," she sobs into me.

I will my arm to move and thankfully it does. Reaching for her hurts like hell, but I weave my fingers into her blonde hair. It's messy and untamed, just the way I like it. Once I'm rewarded with her softness, I show no restraint gripping her hair and right away she looks up at me, blinking a few times and then grabs my face looking deep into my eyes. "Oh, baby," she says in an uneasy tone.

I grunt from the impact of her body as she hugs me, but holding her washes the pain away. "Sssshhhh," I respond in an attempt to calm her. My chest burns, God does it ever. I am weak, but simply holding on to her is the best feeling ever.

Together we just cling to each other, then she pulls away and looks me deep in the eyes. The pain inside of me becomes almost unbearable and Arion begins to panic as she reads it on my face. Reaching over me, she presses the nurse call button.

"It's okay, baby. Just calm down, they'll give you something for the pain."

I nod my head, keeping my eyes focused only on hers, as a nurse comes into the room. She starts to ask Arion what happened, and I do my best to keep my eyes on hers but…

"What happened?" I ask her.

"You passed out from the pain."

"Well, that part I gathered. But, how did I end up in here? I can't remember anything after leaving the house, when I went for a run."

"Really?"

"Yeah."

"Jesus, Bain. That's scary. You were running and you got hit by a car."

"What?" I snap, completely confused and shocked that I cannot remember any of it.

"Yeah, you didn't stop at an intersection. That's when a car hit you."

"It was the pills," I say ashamed, but knowing that I need to be completely honest with her.

"I know, I saw the house, but none of that matters. You're okay now."

"I am, since you're here. Are my injuries bad?"

"Kinda. Thankfully, the car wasn't going very

fast, but you hit your head, which is what knocked you out, and the impact ruptured your spleen."

"Fuck, I can't believe I don't remember any of it," I look down at my body, but it is underneath a blanket, so nothing is visible to me.

"Oh, baby. I'm so, so sorry, but you're alive and you'll be okay.

"I don't understand, how I would have run into an intersection."

"It's my fault, I should have never left. I should have stayed at home like you asked."

"It is *not* your fault. Please don't ever think that. I'm the one who did this."

"Thank you for saying that, but if I was home, none of this would have happened. Please know how sorry I am. I can't tell you how scary this has been, I really thought I was going to lose you. When I got here, your room was empty because you were in surgery, but I didn't know that and I thought the worst."

"Didn't someone tell you that?"

"No, but I didn't stop to let them. Since you were bleeding internally, they had to go in immediately to find out why. After being in there they realized it was your spleen, but it took some time to figure that out, and in the process you lost a lot of blood."

"God, this is just so much to process," I tell her, exhaling loudly.

"It's my fault and I can't apologize enough."

"No, it's not. Plus, it doesn't matter now. You're here and that's what's important. I'm scared to ask what you decided, but I have to know."

"I'm sorry I left. It was wrong and dumb of me, especially since this happened. Nate and I both know where my heart lies and that makes things a lot easier for both of us."

Hearing her say those words spins my world upside down. My breathing becomes quick and the machine to my left starts to beep erratically. *I can't lose her. She chose him.*

"Baby, what's wrong?" she asks me.

With my eyebrows creased and tears welling in my eyes, I can't bring myself to say the words. She grabs my face and looks deep into my eyes. Then a nurse bursts into my room. Arion jumps away from me and I can't help but look at her. She's crying like I am and the nurse takes my attention away from her.

"Bain, I'm Sharon1. What's the matter?"

I blink a few times, willing myself to look away from Arion. "Nothing, I'm okay, just sore."

"That's to be expected. You took a hard hit. Your heart rate is a bit elevated. I'm going to look at your wound, okay?"

I nod my head and look down as the nurse lifts a bandage and examines me. The second I see what she is looking at, I become woozy and let my head fall back, looking at Arion instead. She mouths the words, *I love you* to me and instantly makes everything better.

She has her arms tightly wrapped across her body and is chewing on one of her fingernails.

"I'm going to grab your doctor so he can look you over. I'll be back. I'm glad you're awake."

"Thank you," I briefly respond, watching Arion again. It's like a game of cat and mouse. She's so slow and hesitant coming to me and ultimately that makes me nervous. I want her to run to me, but she doesn't.

"Baby, come here," I order her. "I can't take it any longer, I need to know what you've decided."

She smirks at me and kisses me gently, then says, "Did you ever doubt that I would choose you?"

"Clearly I did. I lost my fucking mind without you."

"Well, I didn't. Deep down from the second I laid eyes on you, I knew that you were my future. You're my everything, Bain. You're all I ever wanted and I was dumb to get clouded in thoughts of my past just because Nate came back."

"Really?" I ask, honestly confused by her confession.

"Yes, really."

"Jesus, I love you, Arion."

"I love you more."

"You know, you said you only needed one more day off and it's been practically two weeks," James jokes with me.

"I know, I'm sorry about that, it's not like I got hit by a car on purpose," I retort humorously.

"I know, I know," he repeats.

I was released from the hospital yesterday

and boy does it feel good to be at home. I'm sore as fuck, but the doctors say that goes with the territory. Glancing out of the corner of my eye, I catch sight of Arion, so breathtaking that my cock and body ache for her. She walks back in with a water for James and sits next to me. So close that she is practically on my lap.

"Don't let me interrupt you two," she says with a smirk on her face.

"You won't. I'm glad that you're here," James adds. "I wanted to talk to both of you about rumors that the Nets are thinking of trading Bain."

"What?" I spit, so angry that I hurt my incision. Pain radiates through me, so harsh my breathing skips a beat. *Traded?* "The season hasn't even started yet, I really don't understand. I was their top pick in the first round."

"The Miami Heat really like you and are willing to make a sweet deal, at least that's what I've heard. I've yet to confirm this with anyone from the Nets organization. I don't want to freak you out, but it's also my job to be honest with you."

I look at Arion as she stares at me with worry etched all across her face. Jesus, if only I could get into her head, even if it was just for a few moments.

"When will you know more?" she asks.

"I'm hoping in the next day or so. This is just part of the business, guys."

"Can I do anything to help?" she asks.

"No, but thank you, Arion. I'll let you know if anything comes up. Listen, I have to run to another meeting. I just didn't want you to get caught off guard when ESPN gets wind of this. I'm hoping your agent might know more than I do. But I'll be in touch. Just take care of yourself, okay?"

I nod my head and give James a hug as he leans down to me. Then he kisses Arion on the cheek and she walks him out.

As she walks back to me on the couch, I do my best to stay positive. Deep down I know no matter what happens, she'll come with me. But in the past we have struggled going down this road. But this is our fate and we have to learn to accept it. We'll be together always and really...that's all that matters.

CHAPTER 15

-Arion-

"Are you okay?" Bain asks me.

Instinctively I nod my head, but inside I'm not really sure. Hearing the news that he might get traded is a shock. I guess none of that should matter. Thinking about the positive side of things, at least he's getting traded and not cut. It doesn't make a difference where he goes – we'll go together and be together.

"Are you okay?" I ask him, scooting softly over beside him. I don't know what it is or why, but since we've been home, I can't seem to get close enough to him.

"Yeah, I mean, what can I do about it? This is life, our life, and what's meant to be will be, baby."

I can't help but smirk at him and then lay my head on his lap. We sit in silence, relishing one another's solace. I thank God for this moment, for Bain and everything that he has given to me. The serenity that surrounds me causes me to close my eyes. Then Bain's phone rings and I hop up to grab it for him. The screen says *private* and I fear it's related to the trial.

Handing the phone to Bain, he hesitates for half a second, then brings it to his ear. "Hello," he answers firmly.

I can't help but watch his face as all of the color drains from it. His confidence and poise are washed away in an instant.

"Okay," he says. "Uh-huh."

He looks at me while he talks and I know what's going on.

"Really? Jesus Christ, okay, we'll be there." He listens for a moment. "No, I'll call them. You don't need to."

He tilts his head back and his tone changes. "Yes, that is still correct. Okay, we'll see you then."

He hangs up, dropping the phone and begins to shake his head slowly. Tears overflow out of his eyes and I reach for him, needing to touch him.

"My parents and I need to testify at the sentencing."

"What? Why?"

"He copped a plea deal."

"I didn't know that."

"Yeah, that was the news I got about the case when you were gone."

"Damn, I'm sorry, baby. How long?"

"Twelve to twenty motherfucking years is all that asshole is getting."

"I don't understand. Last I'd heard the DA was hoping he'd get fifty."

"I don't know either. She said that this judge is really lenient and in order to get the maximum penalty imposed then she's recommending that my parents and I all speak at the sentencing," he says readjusting himself on the couch, pain blazing in his eyes when he moves, and I just feel so bad for him.

"When is it?"

"Next month."

"Well, at least you can heal."

"I told you, baby, I'm fine. I'm home with you and that's all that matters."

"I feel the same way, but I can tell you're still sore." He glares at me and I stop talking about how he is feeling. "Are you going to talk to your parents about this?"

"Yeah, I'll call them, but not now. I know they are both working and I don't want to upset them while they are there. I'll call them tonight."

"Oh yeah, I forgot your mom went back to work. How is she liking it?"

"She loves it, it's a good change for her."

"And you, are you okay with the plea?" I ask, afraid that inside he's a wreck.

"As shitty as it is to know that asshole is basically getting away scot-free, at least he is going to serve some time. I know deep down that Kinsey wouldn't want me to be upset, so I hold on to that."

I smile at Bain and he puckers his lips to me, showing me that he wants a kiss.

Leaning over, I kiss him, tasting his sweetness. His eyes are closed and a growl comes from his throat.

"I think you promised me lunch after James left."

"That I did," I respond and kiss him one last time before walking to our fridge. Looking inside, I realize that I really need to go to the store. "What do you feel like?" I ask and turn to see Bain coming towards me. He's slow to walk, but fuck, he's hot in a pair of basketball shorts and a thin white t-shirt. "Baby, what are you doing up?" I ask.

"I didn't like being away from you and I wanted to watch you cook."

I roll my eyes, grabbing one of the chairs from our kitchen table and pull it over for him to sit on. He kisses my forehead before he not so gracefully flops down. "I don't like how sore you are," I complain.

"I'm fine. It's more my ribs than the incision anyways."

"Do you know when the team doctors will clear you to start practicing?" I ask, taking some food out of the fridge.

"I'm hoping next week."

I glare at him and he leans forward, swatting my ass. I yelp and then notice him hunkered over in pain. Kneeling between his legs, I hold on to him, trying to take away some of the pain. "I'm okay," he responds after a long pause.

"You are not okay. You need to get back to the couch and rest."

Then out of my peripheral vision, I catch sight of his cock, hard and big, straining for attention. He mouths the word "please" to me when I look back at him. I question doing this for only half a second, but figure if I go slow and easy that it *will* be nothing but pleasure. A pleasure both of us have been seeking for a while now. With my signature smirk plastered across my face, I gently pull his shorts down, removing his hard member. With my free hand, I cup his balls and keep the pressure of the fabric from riding up. Then making a few small movements, I look deep into his eyes. It doesn't last long though, my mouth yearns for him like nothing else, so I wrap my soft lips around his thick head, swirling my tongue as I go down on him. He tilts his head back, groaning as I move ever so gently, up and down.

I love the feeling of controlling him like this. I also love that even though I am being gentle, I still please him to this level. Doing this for him makes my pussy burn in anticipation. Fuck, I want him inside of me, but he's too weak. Removing my hand from his shaft, I take him hands-free, clamping my lips tightly around as I go. He reaches for my hair, twisting his fingers into it and I know he is close already.

Without faltering my movements, I keep a steady pace, so thankful that we are both in this moment together.

"Fuck, baby," he growls, letting go with no warning and coming deep in my throat. I relish his deliciousness, swallowing and savoring every bit of him. He smiles at me as I keep going, not wanting to stop. Then he nods his head and says, "Harder."

Reaching up, I clench his cock at the base and quickly pull him in and out of my mouth. To my surprise, it doesn't take but a few quick strokes and he comes again. He makes the most ravenous noises. His hand is still locked tightly in my hair and this time once he's finished, I stop. Afraid that a third come would hurt him. All though I am curious to see if I'd be able to push him there.

CHAPTER 16

-Nate-

"How are you feeling?" my doctor asks me.

"I guess okay."

"Are you sleeping?"

"When I take my meds, I am."

"Any pain in your leg?" he asks as he looks at what is left of my poorly mangled stub of a leg.

"A little. It's more of a dull throbbing pain."

"That's the nerve damage," he responds, hitting both of my knees to check their reflexes. Both of them nudge forward on their own.

"You look good, Nathaniel, minus your weight. I want you to meet with our dietitian and see what you can do to gain forty to fifty pounds.

"Fifty?" I exclaim.

"Yes, fifty. Other than that, you are damn lucky. Your eyes look good, both have healed exceptionally well, and the same goes for your leg. All of the scars look like they have healed great. I think you can start coming in every three months. How does that sound?"

The news is a sigh of a relief. Since all of this started, I have been in and out of the doctors' offices so frequently that finally hearing I am making progress makes me feel good.

"That is…if you can put on some weight," he says before he leaves the room.

"I promise," I respond and shake his hand. He turns on a dime before I can say another word, and the door clicks closed behind him. Quickly, I change out of the pathetic gown, putting my clothes back on and place the referral slip for a prosthetic in my pocket. Jesus, I can't imagine how good it will feel to walk on my own again. It will be a dream come true.

I get in the car and mentally decide to make a detour. I know that any day now will be my last to visit. I think saying goodbye in a proper way will help me to truly move on. I guess I have God to thank for that, even though I don't feel like it. These days, I've been looking for anything to do with my time even if it's hard on me or not, even something that I particularly don't like, because I have to keep busy. Being without

Arion is weighing so heavily on me. It's harder than I ever imagined and I don't know how else to handle things.

My psychologist says for me to let her go. To think back to where we first made a connection and cut it, but that's impossible. Trust me, I've tried.

As I drive down the rows and rows of tomb-stones, I know right where I am headed. When you are going to visit your own grave, how can you get lost? The grass is green, so green, and the trees are tall and fully budded. I put my car in park and collect my crutches, then head out. I stop for a few moments and stand in the bright and warm sun, gathering the heat.

Then I know what I have to do and I will myself to move forward. With every step comes great trials, but this is something that I am doing for myself. I repeat that over and over in my head as many times as I can. Hoping the words will be my strength today.

Finally, kneeling at my grave, my name is clear as day. *Nathaniel Jeffrey Wilcox.*

It's so strange to imagine that my friends and family laid me to rest here, when I was struggling to stay alive halfway across the world. If only they would have known that I'd survived, things now would be so different. Arion wouldn't have fallen in love with someone else. She would have been fighting for my return home, just like I was.

Instead, fate had a different hand of cards laid out for me. Anything I'd ever dreamed of was washed away. My future was erased as if my past never existed. The person I once was vanished, and now here I sit at his grave, trying to make sense of how I ended up in this whole mess of what I call my life.

Today my emotions are replaced with anger. An anger so big and heavy that it scares the shit out of me.

I know any day the military will be removing my grave. It was a mistake in the first place to have it put here, when I am certainly *not* dead. But today something brought me here. I guess inside I wanted to say goodbye. Goodbye to the Nate I used to be. Goodbye to the memories, of him and the person he was. He is long gone and not coming back. Although this is an extremely hard pill to swallow, I have to do it.

Staring at the white headstone, reading my name over and over, I say a silent prayer. Leaving everything I ever knew in the past. I ask God for a sign that what I am doing is right and instantaneously a huge hawk flies over my head, squawking as he does. I look up to see his wings spread wide, a mixture of light and dark. I watch as he silently glides away and wish that could be me. I would give anything in the world to leave my life behind, to be free of my obsession with Arion.

"I'd like to schedule an appointment for a prosthetic."

The woman on the other end of the line rambles on about the process. Then proceeds to tell me how busy they are.

"That's three weeks away...you have got to be kidding me."

I guess it's sooner than not having an appointment at all. "Sure, that'll work," I respond.

We wrap up the call just as there is a knock at the door. I get up and answer it. To my surprise, my utter surprise, it's one of my friends from boot camp. I've talked on the phone with him a few times, but he lives out of state, so to see him here shocks me.

"Nash?" I ask him, just to make sure my eyes aren't deceiving me.

"It's me. How the hell are you?" he asks.

"Uhhh, okay," I say shrugging my shoulders and gesture him inside. He pats me on the back and I close the front door, walking back to the couch. "What brings you to town, man?"

"Actually, I just moved here with my girl-friend."

"No shit. That's awesome. How are things with her?"

"Good, really good. We're getting serious. How about you?"

"I've been better. Things have been hard."

"Did you end up talking to your girl?"

"Yeah, I saw her and we talked."

"And…?" He looks me straight in the eye.

"Let's just say she's not my girl anymore. She's really happy in the relationship she's in."

"Damn, that's horrible, I'm sorry."

"It is what it is. She's not mine, I could sense it all along. I'm just praying that things will change. I'll always love her.

"I'm sorry, bro. I know how much she meant to you. She's all you used to talk about."

"There's nothing that I can do about it. Enough about me, I didn't know your girl lived here," I say changing the subject, in hopes that he won't bring up Arion again.

"She didn't used to, but her work recently transferred her here so I came along for the ride."

"Ahhh, I see. Still not taking life seriously"

"Oh, I am. I'm going to open a gym; I just have to find the right space. Speaking of which, you should come with me and work out sometime."

I can't contain the laugh inside of me. I am in no shape to be in a gym. I couldn't imagine the way that people would stare at me. "I think I'm probably the last person that you should ask to work out with."

"Why?" he asks me point blank.

"Uhhhh, because of my leg. Plus, I've been lifting some dumbbells here and it's been a struggle."

"Nate, I don't give a shit about your leg and you shouldn't either." I nod my head looking down at myself. "Nate, tell me what it is that you do every day?"

Breaking eye contact with him, I look

around. "Uhhh, it depends on the day. I have a lot of doctors appointments and—"

He cuts me off. "Don't bullshit me. I can see it in your eyes you're lying."

His accusation makes me feel extremely nervous and I'm not sure how to handle the question honestly. All I do is obsess over Arion and how much I miss her.

"You don't have to bullshit me. When I got kicked out of boot camp, it was hard to handle and that doesn't even compare to what you're going through. All I'm getting at is I'm your friend and I wanna help. You've told me yourself that you'd love to gain some weight. I can help you do that."

"Thank you, Nash. I really appreciate that, but I can't go into a gym like this. I have an appointment to get fitted for a prosthetic in three weeks. Once I have that, I promise I'll give it a shot."

"I'll hold you to that."

CHAPTER 17

-Bain-

"Dude, you were off the chain today," LJ, one of my teammates, tells me as we change after practice.

"Thanks, bro."

"Yeah, for sure, glad to have you back."

"Thanks, man, I'll see ya later." Throwing my bag over my shoulder, I make my way out, but hear my name before I can exit. *Dammit, I just wanna get home.* Yeah, I might have played well, but I am sore as fuck.

"Good job today, Adams," the shooting coach says as I turn around. He waves and continues walking.

"Thanks," I say and continue on my way. I'm still confused by the staff here. Everyone has been super friendly since my return and not one person has said a word about the rumored trade to Miami.

James hasn't called me with any news either. So I guess the motto "No news is good news" applies. Walking into the underground parking garage, there are rows and rows of town cars all lined up to take players home. I guess it's a perk of living in New York City. Walking to Carl's car, he smiles at me and asks, "How are you feeling?"

"Tired. Sore. Exhausted."

"Well, sit back and relax. I think you have a relaxing weekend ahead of you."

His comment throws me off. How would he know what I am doing this weekend? Then he opens the door and my jaw slams against the pavement. "Hi, baby," Arion says, dressed sexy as fuck and patting the seat next to her.

"What are you doing here?" I ask looking between her and Carl.

"Mr. Adams, I just listen to the orders of the missus. You really should get in if you wanna miss traffic out of the city."

Still shocked and not able to really say much, I slide in next to Arion. She's quite leggy in a pair of white shorts and what I wouldn't consider to be a top.

"How was practice?" she asks, grabbing my

hand and kissing it softly.

"It was fine," I respond with my eyebrows scrunched looking at her, trying to get a read on her. "What the hell is going on?"

"I came to pick you up from work, is that okay?"

"Of course it is, but you've never done it before and why did Carl say we need to get going to beat traffic."

"Oh, I booked us a beach house in the Hamptons, is that all right with you?"

"Uhhh, of course, but you know I have to be back in the city on Monday for practice."

"I know. Carl is going to come and pick us up."

"Why did you do this?" I ask turning my body more towards her.

"Because your birthday is tomorrow, silly."

Holy shit, I totally spaced my own birthday. My mind has been so consumed with other things, from Nate, to the accident, to the impending sentencing for Kinsey's killer. I guess it was the farthest thing from me.

"Jesus, you're amazing, you know that, right?"

She nods her head and I can't stop myself

from taking my hands and grabbing her face. Staring deep into each other's eyes, I realize just how goddamn lucky I am. She is absolutely perfect in every way.

"Keep your eyes closed."

"I am, I am," I respond, loving how good her small hands feel pressed so firmly against my eyes. Well, that and her body behind me.

"Okay, kneel down."

"Ohhhh, yes, ma'am," I respond, dropping to my knees. She giggles and then says, "I'm gonna remove my hands, but don't open your eyes yet, okay?"

I nod my head. All of my senses are hypersensitive. I hear her little feet pad softly across the room. "Come here, baby," she whispers and I wonder if she is talking to me.

Then she says, "Keep 'em closed, Bain."

"I am, I am."

"You can sit all the way down if you want."

"Nah, I like kneeling for you."

She chuckles. "Put your hands out." Reaching forward, still with my eyes closed, I pray that I get her naked body.

"What the fuck, did you forget to shave?" I feel a lot of hair in my hands.

"No, open them." I open my eyes and in front of me is a puppy. "Happy birthday, baby."

Looking at the small creature in my hands, I am a little unsure how to react. As I sit staring at him, he does the same to me with his little, black face and green eyes.

"Does he move?" I ask her.

"Yeah, he's just sleepy from the car ride. I gave him a Benadryl."

"You drugged my dog?" I accuse her sarcastically.

"I needed to surprise you."

"Fine, I guess that's okay," I tell her kissing her sweet lips.

"Do you like him?"

"I love him. Are you sure you're going to be okay with a dog so soon after losing Zeus?"

Tears gloss over her eyes as she looks at me and she says, "Yeah, I'll be good. Thank you for being concerned."

"Of course," I say petting the little guy.

"Ahhh, I knew you would love him. He's

funny as fuck when he's not drugged."

"Oh God, is he crazy?"

"No, he's actually chill and really clumsy. I think he's afraid of socks. He tripped on one of yours at the house and I tried to play with him with it and he hid from me."

"He's so perfect. Thank you, baby. How did I not see him in the car?"

"He was up front with Carl. That's why I asked him to drive us. That and I figured it would give us some alone time."

"Well, you should have told Carl to get a limo so I could have fucked you."

"Yes, I'm sure he would have appreciated that. So what do you want to do this weekend?"

"Be with you and this guy," I tell her as our pup lies down between us.

"Good, I had the fridge stocked so we shouldn't need to leave at all. There's a hot tub and obviously we are close to the beach."

"Thank you, Arion, for everything. I love you so much."

"And I…I love you."

Lifting my hand, she stands and I follow suit. "What about the dog?"

"He'll sleep, trust me," she says, pulling her

shirt over her head. She has no bra on and I get a full view of her bare back. Even knowing what she looks like when she turns around, still doesn't calm my dick. It's hard and pulsating against my pants. Then she drops her pants and has no underwear on either. I get a full view of her ass as she turns towards me at the foot of the master bed.

"You're next," she tells me, reaching between her legs and pleasing herself. She knows that's my job. So as fast as I can, I undress and then change my tune. Rather than charging towards her like a caveman, I reach down and clench my cock, gripping hard at the base and pulling towards the end. She blinks a few times, caught off guard, tilting her head and slowing her movements.

"How does it feel?" I ask her, not stopping myself. I need to teach her a lesson. I hate it when she does this, so she needs to know how it feels.

She finally stops and then answers me. "I don't like it."

"What don't you like? Touching yourself or me touching myself."

"You," she shrieks and lunges towards me,

dropping to her knees. I don't let go of myself, instead I grip hard, guiding my dick into her sweet mouth.

"Mmm, you suck a damn good cock." Her lips are stretched so pink and bright. When I tilt my head to the right, I see one of her tits perfectly. It causes me to let go and reach down for her nipple. She moans when I tweak it, taking me deep in her throat. She shows no mercy as she sucks me, clearly trying to prove a point.

I stay still, letting her prove whatever it is that she needs to. Not only because she's so sexy naked on her knees, but because I'm about to come. I try and refrain from doing so, not wanting to let go so soon, but then she does it, she takes me all the way in, gripping my ass as she does and touching her nose against my skin.

My body shivers with pleasure, causing my cock to become rock hard. Moving my hand to her face, I caress her beautiful skin. She has her eyes closed and is loving this as much as I am. I cup the back of her head, no longer able to stay still, moving my hips, I gently buck into her mouth and let go. Grunting like a caveman and all, but I don't care. She moans in return telling me that she likes it and takes all that I give her. I finally settle, coming back down to reality, but she's not stopping. The sensation is too great, so I'm forced to pull away.

Through those sexy, light eyes, she smirks at me. "What?" I ask.

"I just love you. That's all."

"And I love you," I respond, reaching down and scooping her up. She giggles a little as I carry her to the bed. *No, fuck the bed.* Instead, I set her sexy ass on top of the dresser. She spreads her legs for me, her pink pussy glistening with wetness and I nudge my throbbing member against her opening. She looks at me as our bodies are so close, not quite one, but close to molding together.

Her eyes dance with anticipation and in that moment my restraint becomes very weak. My body moves on its own, not caring that I want to play with her. Filling her with my cock, she's so tight, and once I'm nuzzled in all the way, I am home. This is my heaven.

Letting her legs relax over my arms. I hold on to her back and begin moving, deep, hard, purposeful thrusts. Arion lets her head fall back, crying out my name. Watching her relinquish everything over to me turns me on so much. She always wants what I have to give, no matter what. Uncontrollably, I begin slamming into her. Her legs fall down as I pick up speed. My body is covered in pleasure. From head to toe, this is what she does to me. Even though I just came, she takes me there so quickly.

With each thrust, I watch her pink nipples bounce up and down. She looks at me, her lip tucked so tightly in between her teeth. "Are you gonna come on my cock?" I ask.

"Ahhh, fuck, yes," she responds, letting go, and I watch a sheen of sweat cover her body. Then, almost out of nowhere, I feel my own release. It completely catches me off guard. Rather than fight it like I normally do, I relish it. Tilting my head back, savoring the last of her orgasm noises while I let her pussy take me where it wants.

Pure bliss takes over and a powering orgasm washes through me. Once I finally open my eyes, Arion is watching me with that cute ass smirk on her face. Smirking right back, I lift her up and carry her to the bed, where we lie down together. Well, more like me in her arms, but this is my paradise. This is where I feel the most comfortable. "Thank you for this," I tell her. Then I hear faint footsteps. So light that they are hard to make out, but I know right away who they belong to. Glancing at the entrance of the bedroom, I catch a glimpse of my new pup. His ears are back and he is clearly nervous. Arion lifts her head and looks at him. "Isn't he cute?" she asks me.

I nod my head, then call him over to us. Right away his attitude changes, he flies across the room, sliding on the hardwood floor the entire way. I can't help but laugh at him. Rolling over, I pick him up, noticing how he must already weigh thirty pounds.

His ears go back when I touch him, and then the moment I set him down, he rewards me with puppy kisses. "Ahhh, he likes you," she says.

"Stop, stop," I tell him putting my hand in front of my face. He plops his butt down and glares at me as if I've insulted him.

"So what do you want to name him?" she asks.

"I have no idea, I'm not good with that stuff. Don't you have any ideas?"

"A few, yes, but I thought you would too."

"What about Guy? He's a cute little guy, right?"

"No!" she shrieks and slaps me on the back of my head.

"Ow," I shout, rubbing where she just hit. "Sorry, it's all I got."

"No. Absolutely, not, NO! We are not calling him Guy. How about Diego?"

"Arion, this isn't Dora the Explorer, this is real life."

"Hmmmm, how about Norelco?"

"What? He's not a razor. You said you had ideas."

"I do, let me think."

"You are acting really blonde right now, be careful what you say."

"Am not," she says, glaring at me. "What should we name you, little buddy?" she asks looking the dog square in the eyes. "Buddy!" she exclaims.

"That's it, his name is Guy. He's my birthday gift, so I get to choose. For your birthday I'll get you a dog and you can name it Cupcake or Sparkles or Tupperware or whatever. Isn't that right, Guy?" He leans into my touch and lies down next to me.

"'Guy?' Really? Why don't you just call him Man or Dude."

"No, it's Guy," I tell her, pinning her beneath me.

She smiles and drops our conversation, surrendering over to me, the way she always does. My lips find hers and right away...I am lost...lost in all that she is and all that we are.

CHAPTER 18

-*Arion*-

Everything is going to be fine, stop freaking out. Even though I repeat the words in my head, it still doesn't matter. I've arranged for everyone closest to Bain to meet us for his birthday dinner and he has no idea. He thinks it'll just be the two of us, and for some reason, I am really nervous. I mean, I don't want to screw things up and I'm not good with surprises.

Looking over myself one last time in the mirror, I'm in a tight, gold dress, that's so not my style, but Bain fell in love with it when we went shopping, so I bought it for the occasion. Walking to the bedroom window, I see Bain and Guy out front of the beach cottage. Bain is calling Guy over to him and he walks with his bright green ball tucked tightly in his mouth. Then he puts his head down and his butt in the air, wagging his tail fiercely. Watching those two together reminds me of how Nate used to be with Zeus. It really saddens me that Zeus died. But in all honesty, I wasn't the best mom to him.

Quickly I'm pulled out of my mindfuck when I see Bain fall as he's chasing Guy. Sand goes flying, but he doesn't care. When everything finally settles, Bain has the ball. He is dressed for dinner, but you can tell he doesn't care as he lies there and lets Guy walk all over him. I knew Bain wanted a dog, but I had no idea that it would make him this happy.

I text James to make sure everything is good to go for dinner. Right away he responds that we are all set and I head out front. As I open the door, Bain is brushing himself off and he looks up at me as I walk down the stairs.

"You are absolutely breathtaking. You know that?"

"Well, thank you, I could say the same about you. Minus the sand in your hair," I tell him, reaching up to brush it away.

He wraps one arm around me, then tosses the ball he had in the other, before fully engulfing me in his warmth and his scent. God, I love everything about him.

Guy goes running off and I don't waste one second pressing my lips hard against Bain's. He smiles looking down at me, as he kisses me back, then his eyes close and I watch as the beast within starts to show more aggression, passion, and love. My heart pounds hard against my chest, until Guy slams into me, almost knocking me over. Bain catches me and we both laugh at the little ball of fur staring up at us.

"Are you sure he can't come to dinner?" Bain asks me.

"Babe, what do you think?"

"I know, I know, he's just so much fun."

"He'll be fine for a few hours, especially with how much the two of you have played today."

"True. Are you ready to get going?"

"Yup, we have six o'clock reservations. I just need to put my heels on."

Bain looks down at his watch, and immediately I see the panic on his face. He hates being late, to anything. I, on the other hand, don't mind so much. Plus, all I need to do is text James and let him know when we arrive. He said everyone is going to get there early and have a few drinks anyways. Bain and I head towards the house while Guy follows right behind us.

Looking back, his head is held high and he is just sniffing the air.

Both Bain and I just smirk at each other, that is until Guy runs smack into the stairs leading up to the house and looks a bit stunned. The hit plops him right on his butt and he shakes his head. Bain laughs, picking him up, and carries him to his kennel. "You're a goofy little guy," he tells him, giving him one last pat on the head.

We lock up and head down the driveway, right on time like I scheduled, our limo is waiting for us.

"You're the best, baby, thank you," Bain says, kissing me behind my ear.

"Of course, how else would we get to dinner?"

"A cab?"

"We're not in the city and it's your day, remember?"

The driver is a nice middle-aged female who welcomes us by opening the door and wishing Bain happy birthday. "You are going to love this place, baby," Bain says. "They have the best seafood."

"As long as I'm with you, I'm sure I will. Is there anything that you want to do before we head back in the morning?"

"Just this," he responds, kissing my neck and chest. The driver rolls the dividing window up and Bain pulls away, looking behind him. Then he slides his fingers into the fabric of my dress, caressing my breast while paying extra attention to one of my nipples. I throw my head back, biting my bottom lip and am so happy that I don't have a bra on. Bain is eager, I can tell looking down and catching sight of his huge cock straining against the fabric of his pants. I go to reach for Bain, but he stops me, claiming my lips between his. Moving one of his hands, he trails it all the way down my body, 'til he reaches between my legs. Like he loves, I have no underwear on, complete commando. A growl brews, silent at first, then builds as he looks up at me.

Without wasting another second, he unzips his pants, releasing his cock, then pushes himself towards my opening. "Lift your dress up," he orders through heavy breaths. I do so, my body full of adrenaline and desire. As Bain begins to fill me, he also connects our mouths, invading mine with his tongue while his dick begins to move into me.

The second that he is nestled to the hilt, he pulls his mouth away from mine and looks at me. "Are you going to come?" he asks me with a smirk.

I nod my head, looking into his sexy, light eyes, so turned on that we are doing this in the back of a limo. Holding himself up, Bain moves in and out calculatedly, causing my body to become flooded with the greatest sensations. I can't help but look down, moving my dress a little so I can see his hard cock moving in and out of me.

Fuck, that has to be the hottest thing I've ever seen. "You like that, don't you?" Bain asks me breathlessly, watching exactly what I am.

"God, yes," I cry out, completely surrendering to him. Then he moves his hands, bracing the back of the seat, and shows no mercy as he crashes into me. I want to scream, but I hold back, closing my eyes, letting my body enjoy the building of the sensation. My world begins to spiral, the most marvelous feeling. I tighten my pussy muscles hard and Bain grunts out violently. Reaching up, I clamp my hand over his mouth and watch as he comes deep inside me. My body no longer can resist and I let go, spiraling, spinning, and twirling every which way.

Pure, candid bliss covers me. Everything rocks from my head to my toes and I enjoy every last minute of it. Finally, I come back to reality. Looking at the sexiest man alive. He kisses my nose then pulls his cock out of me. Reaching for a few tissues, he hands them to me. "Thank you," I respond, cleaning myself up.

"Thank you," he says adjusting himself back into his pants, then reaches for the chilled bottle of champagne and asks, "Is this for us?"

I nod my head, watching him untwist the wrapping around the cork. He smiles pointing it at me. "You wouldn't dare," I tell him.

"Oh, I would. But only if you were bent over and it was sure to hit your ass."

"Bain," I screech, putting my hands up to block him. He tilts the bottle down and I really begin to get nervous. He wouldn't...would he?

Then he points it straight up and the cork flies to the ceiling, crashing hard. I smirk at him, watching him take two champagne flutes in one hand and so gracefully fill them while the car takes a turn. He sets the bottle back in the ice and hands me a glass, getting particularly close to me.

Looking into my eyes, he stares before saying anything.

"I love you so much," I tell him.

"I love you, Arion. I don't think I've told you with everything that's happened and gone on, but thank you. Thank you for making me the happiest man alive and for choosing me. I honestly could not live without you. You are my angel and a blessing."

Tears gloss over my eyes as we clink our glasses. He's never really said anything like that to me before. Taking a small sip, I look at him and know I made the right decision, without a doubt. I am 100% confident that Bain is the only one for me.

CHAPTER 19

-Nate-

Fuck, her lips are so good, so soft. I've waited forever for her to kiss me like this. Kissing her back, I look down at her naked, precious body, not waiting another second before sinking my cock inside.

As my flesh touches her, she gasps and I wonder how in God's name I lasted this long without her. My breathing is dense; I don't want to fuck this up. But her eyes tell me that everything is okay, so I proceed. Loving how her tight, pink cunt feels against my skin, like a vice around me. Gently, I begin moving, savoring our time together...

Looking down, I blink a few times, Arion is not with me. My hand is clenched around my dick, and it's hard and throbbing. Letting my head fall back, the sickness that is my life takes over. What am I going to do without her? I release some of the tension in my hand, but notice right away how good it feels to keep a tight grip, so I hold myself harder. Closing my eyes, I begin to move my hand and for the first time in a long time, I let myself enjoy the pleasure.

My mind races and I go back to my dream, Arion's body so perfectly laid beneath mine. I can still picture every little detail about her. From the way her lips part when she pants during sex to how her body bows giving into the sensation.

Picturing her like that is the biggest turn on, and I jerk myself hard, already close to climax. My balls bounce with each movement and I pray to God neither of my parents catch me. But the feeling is too great, a wave of pleasure takes over. The need to come so immense, that my body burns and I let go, envisioning only those sweet lips around my cock as I release. However, my reality is quickly put into check. There are no lips. She is not here and…she never will be.

Though the feeling was amazing, and something I've been deprived of for quite some time, it is quickly washed away. Now here I lie in the pathetic, pain-staking reality that is my existence. Sitting up, I take my shirt off and clean myself, then decide to get up and take a quick shower, because the moment I lie back down, everything is too painful.

The shower doesn't help. I'm not sure what I was hoping it would do, but for some reason, today things just seem…harder. I'm angrier and feel more hopeless than ever. Looking down at my pathetic stub of a leg, I can't wait for my prosthetic appointment. Maybe that will help me a little more. Maybe if I could walk on my own and help myself the way I used to, I would start to feel like the old me.

As I sit on the edge of my bed and dry myself, my cell phone vibrates. Looking at the screen, I notice it's Nash. I answer it, knowing anything at this point will take my mind off of Arion and the depression I seem to be in today.

"What's up, bro?" he says in his usual chipper tone.

"Not much, just getting going for the day. You?"

"I'm about to go look at this sick spot for a gym, wanna come?"

My automatic response is no and then I look around my room. Realizing I have absolutely nothing better to do today. "Where is it?"

"North Jersey, so it's a bit of a drive, but I'm

almost to your house, so we should be able to make good time if you're ready."

"What? You're already on your way?"

"Yeah, is that a problem?"

"What if I say no?"

"You won't. Trust me, I know you. You were probably waiting for something to do today."

"You're an ass."

"I know. Now get your sexy ass ready and you better be waiting on the curb for me."

"Don't call me sexy, you fucking weirdo, and I won't wait on the curb for anyone."

"Fine, I'll pull in the driveway. But be ready, I'll be there in ten."

Hanging up, I wonder what in God's name I'm getting myself into. He's the polar opposite of me. He's wild and outgoing, and that's…just not me. But it doesn't matter. He's really been my only friend through all of this. Yes, maybe it's because everyone still thinks I'm dead…minor hindrance on the social life.

I get dressed and head downstairs. My mom is in the kitchen making coffee. She looks tired, more so today than she has lately. But catching her up and in the kitchen makes me feel good. I know her seeing me all up and at 'em is what puts that bright smile on her face. "Hey, honey," my mom tells me, pulling a chair out for me at the table.

"Thanks, Ma. I actually can't sit. Nash is picking me up this morning. He needs me to look at a place for the new gym he's opening."

"Oh, that's great news. I've always liked Nash."

I can't help but laugh under my breath. He has totally pulled the wool over my mom's eyes. Then out front I hear his horn and kiss my mom on the cheek.

"Take care of yourself today, okay, Ma?"

She nods her head and I walk off. Looking back at her as I close the door, she has tears in her eyes. I know it kills her to see me like this, but this is the person that I am now. I close the door grateful that she didn't follow me all the way out. Recently I asked her to give me some space and let me do some things on my own. Clearly, it is hard for her, but she's doing well respecting me.

Nash has the music blaring in his huge truck. I just smirk as I walk to it and the first thought that crosses my mind is how in the world am I going to get into something so tall? It's massive.

Then the door flies open and I know obstacle number one is covered. Now, I don't have to reach up and balance to open the door on one leg. He turns the music down and says to me, "You look so small down there. We really gotta get you on a workout regimen."

"Hello to you too," I tell him tossing my crutches in the back. Then with all of my strength, I brace my weight and hop up into his beast of a vehicle.

"You know I'm just fucking with you, right?" he says, backing out of my driveway.

"Does it matter? It's the truth. I need to do something about my weight."

"You know, man, I'm more than happy to help."

"We'll see," I respond. "I'm getting my prosthetic soon and I think that will help with my motivation."

"Cool."

"So where's this place?"

"Up north, in an industrial part of town, but not far from a suburb and the train into the city, so I really think there is potential with all of the commuters that work there."

"So what's your overall goal?"

"In no more than three months, I want the doors open to my own gym."

"Wow, that's really fast."

"I know, but if I don't put those deadlines on myself, it will never get done."

"Why a gym? I don't remember you being so into working out."

"I wasn't 'til I broke up with Erica. It was the only thing that got me off of the couch and made me feel remotely good about myself."

"I'm sorry, man."

"It's okay. That's why I think you would benefit from it."

The rest of the drive we talk and reminisce. Hanging out with Nash like this reminds me why I became friends with him in the first place. He is genuine and just wants what is best for those closest to him.

It's not long 'til Nash turns down a short alley and then parks, looking up at the building. "This is it," he says.

I look up as well at the all-brick industrial building. Then we get out and Nash is greeted by who I guess is the realtor. "I'm Amesha," she says, shaking his hand then mine. She must be in her twenties and is absolutely gorgeous. Right away I get embarrassed, standing here with one leg and skinny as fuck. That's why I need to make a change, if I ever want Arion to look at me. I'm going to begin working out with Nash. I mean...I have to.

Heading through the back door, I follow Nash and Amesha listening to her explain all of the details about the building. It's over five thousand square feet and one massive open space. Looking at Nash, there is a huge grin on his face. I can tell that this is exactly what he wants.

"So what do you think?" she asks Nash.

"I love it. What do you think, Nate?" he asks me.

"It's awesome."

"Good," Amesha says. "There's just one problem. The owner has decided he only wants to sell. I know when we discussed this place, we talked about you renting it."

"Ahh, shit. Really?"

"Yes, I'm sorry. He just called me on the drive, and I pleaded with him, but he's going through a divorce and has to. What's your opinion on buying?"

"I don't know if I can. With all of the money

I have saved and the loan I'm prequalified for, that's just enough for the equipment. I'm not sure I could get another loan. How much is he asking anyways?"

"Five hundred thousand."

"Damn, okay. Well, as much as I love this place, and believe me I really do, it's just not gonna work."

"Again, I'm sorry, Nash. I'll keep looking and we'll find you the right spot."

He nods his head and we shake Amesha's hand. I can see the despair all over his face, laced into his eyes.

We get back into his truck and he turns the music off the second it starts. "I'm sorry, man," I tell him, wishing I could make things better.

"Thanks, Nate, sorry I wasted your time today."

"You didn't waste my time. You didn't at all. Thanks for having me along."

"This just blows, man. That place is perfect."

"I know."

Sitting against the leather of the seat, I look over at Nash as we begin our trek home and realize maybe I *can* help him. The military has given me a ton of money that frankly I have no purpose for. I guess to them it was the price on the ten months I was missing and all that I endured. But to me, there is no amount of money that can compensate for what I went through. Looking at Nash and how down he is, I decide the best thing I can do is help him.

"I'll buy the gym for you."

He turns his head faster than I've ever seen him move before, then puts his eyes back on the road when I nod my head yes, to tell him that I'm serious.

"No way, man, I can't have you spend your money like that."

"It's not my money, it's the government's. And to be honest with you, I could use something to focus on, maybe we can work out some sort of partnership."

"I would love that. You would really do this with me?"

"I would, but on one condition."

"Fuck, man, you name it, anything."

"I want you to get me back up to my old weight and to build the muscle I've lost."

"Dude, I'm doing that anyways. What else?"

"Nothing, I don't want anything," I tell him.

CHAPTER 20

-Bain-

"Baby, it's going to be all right. Just take some deep breaths, okay?"

Arion's words are loud and clear, but comprehending what she is asking of me is a whole other thing. We are in the car driving to the courthouse and I know in order to get through today, it will take every last ounce of strength I have.

We've met with the DA, so both my parents and I are ready to speak at the sentencing. However, actually doing it is a whole different story. As Arion turns my BMW off of the freeway, she grabs my hand. She is so confident and strong, just what I need today.

"Are you sure you don't want to eat your bagel?" she asks me, eyeballing the brown paper bag we picked up with our favorite breakfast sandwiches in it.

I shake my head, squeezing her hand a little tighter. My stomach is a ball of fire. I wouldn't wish today on my worst enemy – ever. She holds me tightly back and we get closer and closer to our arrival.

"Have you talked to your parents?"

I glance at my phone and notice that neither of them have called or texted me. "No, I'm sure they are running late, but they'll be there."

Within a few minutes we are parked. Arion looks over at me, cupping my cheek and says, "I love you, Bain. You can do this. Stay strong for Kinsey, okay?"

Leaning over I kiss her lips and then my phone chimes. It's a text from my dad. *We are running a few minutes late. Your mom is struggling this morning and it was hell to get her out of the house. But we'll be there, save us a seat. I love you, son.*

I will, love you guys.

"My parents are running late."

"I'm sure it's been hard for them too."

"Yeah," I respond staring up into the grey clouds.

"Are you ready to head in?" Arion asks me.

I nod my head and get out of the car. I can

do this. I have to…for Kinsey. Arion wraps her hand around mine and I keep my eyes to the ground letting her lead me inside the courthouse, where our final destination will be to spend who knows how long with a monster.

"Bain," she whispers and I look up. The outside of the building is littered with news reporters and camera crews. I know right away what she is referring to. Then I hear my name when one of them spots us as we approach. *"Mr. Adams, Mr. Adams"* is all that echoes in my head.

Both Arion and I stay quiet like we have vowed to. Unless it's a reporter at one of my games, we don't talk. Quickly we walk up the front steps to the courthouse and I do my best to keep my ears closed and just go. Then a question that makes absolutely no sense for today and what we are about to do is asked. "How do you feel about the rumored trade to Miami?"

Annoyance brews inside of me. How could someone be so callous to ask something like that with what I am obviously dealing with today? It completely catches me unprepared and apparently Arion too. She can't help herself and handles it like the little spitfire that she is.

"Are you fucking kidding me?" she snaps,

looking the guy straight in the eye. He is taller than she is, but that doesn't make her back down. "That's your question? On a day when the murderer of his sister is getting sentenced, you wanna know how he feels about being traded? You are fucking unbelievable."

Her rant has quieted the swarm of reporters and stunned me a bit. She glares at him and then tugs my hand and I follow, staring at her a bit in awe. I'm so damn proud that she is mine. When we enter the courthouse, a rush of warmth hits us. It's a cold, cloudy day today, and I know rain is looming nearby. It suits my mood perfectly.

"Are you okay?" she asks me.

"Yeah, thank you for standing up to those reporters."

"Baby, it's my job. You deserve nothing but peace and respect today. That asshole wasn't giving it to you, so I needed him to know that it wasn't okay. I also know your parents are right behind us and I pray to God they leave them alone and don't ask any questions."

"After what you just said, I doubt it."

We arrive at the courtroom and sit on one of the brown, wooden benches, holding each other's hands while we wait for my parents, both of us being quiet. Being with Arion calms me, in a way that no other person in the world can. I know we are about to walk into a shit-storm, but if I have her, I know I'll survive.

"Bain." I recognize my mom's voice right away. Looking up, she is running to me. I stand, engulfing her in a tight hug, and she cries into the fabric of my teal shirt. It was Kinsey's favorite color and I wore it in honor of her today. When my dad is close enough, he hugs Arion, and then the both of them hug my mom and I. As we stand there together, I sense Kinsey's arms shrouded around all of us.

She is with us today – I know it.

Our hug is cut short by the DA. She comes out of the courtroom clearing her throat and we all disperse, but still keep our arms around each other.

"How are you all doing today?" she asks.

"As good as to be expected," my dad tells her.

"Good. Listen, I wanted to let you know that they bumped our time up thirty minutes. So it's go time. Are you guys ready?"

My dad and I nod our heads. To the left of me is Arion and to the right is my mom. She is fragile in her current state, but we have to go through this for Kinsey and she knows that.

Cindie, the DA, heads inside and we follow. The courtroom is old and needs a remodel. The white walls and heavy, dark wood are not comforting. On one side there are only a few people, I'm assuming the family of this asshole.

The other side is packed, a clear congregation of support. Everyone is in teal, showing they are here for Kinsey.

Cindie directs us to sit in the front row. All is quiet while we wait, then a door on the side of the room opens. Two officers walk out with this motherfucker shackled like the fucking pig that he is.

My body tenses as I see Anthony. How could he do this to her? I squeeze my mother and Arion's hands so hard, I'm surprised they sit quietly. In this moment, I can almost envision myself climbing over this wall and killing him with my bare hands. I could snap his little motherfucking neck before anyone was on me.

My body begins to tremble as my thoughts carry me away to a deep, dark place. Then Arion touches my face and it pulls me out of my hallucination. I was mere inches away from snapping. I know in the back of my mind, this could be my only chance to hurt him like I so badly want to – need to. I lean into Arion's touch, letting the tears rolls down my cheeks and just close my eyes. I have to pull myself together. He won't be responsible for my life ending too.

"All rise for the honorable Judge Jenkins," the court clerk announces. We stand and I'm weak in my knees. I can't bear to stay in this moment, and trying not to pass out, I close my eyes praying to Kinsey for help.

When we all sit back down, I lean into Arion, knowing it will help to calm me, and I do everything possible to keep my mind busy. *Whatever you do, don't look at him again* I tell myself, knowing it would make it worse. Then clear as day, I hear Kinsey say to me. *I love you, Bain, I'm all right.* I can picture her saying the words with her long, brown hair messy as always and her calm demeanor. She never cared about her looks and was always confident and free-spirited. Just like the time we went white water rafting for our eighteenth birthday. I was scared, but not her...

"Come on, Bain, you said you wanted to do this," *Kinsey whines as the raft is being loaded with all of the crazy people that signed up to do this, and for some God*

unknown reason, here I stand second-guessing everything.

"I do. I mean, I did."

"Jesus, you're such a baby. Today is our birthday so get your ass in the raft."

"I don't want us to die."

"Nothing is going to happen. Come on, you big baby," she says, reaching her hand out for mine. I look down at it and then take hers and walk to the edge of the water. The guide helps her in the raft and then I follow. She sits there with the biggest smile on her face. It seems to spans from ear to ear. I'd walk across the earth to give her that, so I know I've made the right choice.

"This is gonna be so fun," she says...

"Adams," is the only word that I hear. It takes me a few moments to come back to reality. When I do, my dad is at the stand. He looks scared, even nervous. Which is not something I've ever seen from him. He is usually so confident and poised, ready to take on the world. But today, he is broken. As he begins to speak, my mom begins to sob sitting next to me. I wrap my arm around her and keep her close.

She turns away from the sight of my father and into my shirt. Her cries drown him out for the most part, but not everything. "It kills me every day to think that the gift she could have given the world was taken away. Her life was taken away like it was an ant walking on the sidewalk that you step on. So fast and with no warning. It was taken away at the hands of a monster who sits amongst us in this room."

He pauses briefly composing himself, and my mom cries harder. Arion keeps a tight hold on my hand, now resting her face against the outside of my shoulder.

"My family and I were asked here today to speak on behalf of Kinsey, because she can no longer do that for herself. Now, I'm not her so I don't know what she would say, but if it was up to me, I would kill Anthony Eldridge. So Judge Jenkins I am begging you with everything I am and everything that Kinsey was. Please punish this degenerate to the most severe standards."

He turns and walks to us with fire in his eyes, the previous pain that was on his face no longer there. He opens his arms to my mom as my name is called and she falls against his chest. Arion squeezes my hand as I get up. "I love you," she whispers.

I smile and head to the stand, my eyes locked on Anthony's profile. But, he looks forward, never glancing in my direction. The judge asks me to make my statement and as much as I want to look at Anthony the entire time, to somehow make him feel uncomfortable or to feel the pain that she did, I don't. It will only take my focus off of what I have to say and today is about convincing the judge into giving him the harshest sentence possible.

"Your Honor, thank you for letting me talk today." She smiles at me and I take a deep breath, praying that I can hold it all together.

"My sister, Kinsey, was my best friend. She was an exceptional person. Very sweet, loving, caring, and just amazing all around. She was such a free spirit, I've never met anyone quite like her. She loved life. Every single second of every day was a new adventure for her. And now that Kinsey is gone from this earth that she loved, the world is not the same, especially through my family's eyes. The way we breathe isn't the same, the way we think isn't the same, even the people that we are today aren't the same as we were when Kinsey was alive. Everything is different, not only for us, but so many others. I mean, look at all of the people in this room today wearing her favorite color. Each and every one of their lives has been affected by her loss and the only person to blame is Anthony Eldridge." I stop and look at him; he still stares off into the courtroom. It's like he's drugged or something. "Anthony went as far as to stage her death as her suicide. The way he made it look changed what people thought of Kinsey and that's not fair for so many reasons. He portrayed her to be someone different than who she was. All along, I knew it wasn't true. I knew there was no way that she took her own life. It had to be at the hands of another person, a disgusting individual. Anthony Eldridge is that miscreant. He is a sick, twisted person that has changed all of our lives for the worst. He murdered her, plain and simple. How, we will never know, as he hasn't told us and she was cremated, destroying any evidence. Not knowing what really happened to her is absolutely heartbreaking. But regardless, Anthony has pled guilty, so I'm begging you, your Honor, with every ounce of the man that I am, and as Kinsey's twin brother, to please sentence him to the fullest degree of the law."

"Thank you, Mr. Adams," the judge says.

I nod my head and sit down, my body trembling from my heart beating so hard against my chest. I made it through one of the hardest parts of this. As hard as it was to do it – I did it. My poor mom is still a sobbing mess. I know there is no way she can get up and speak to the judge. However, I'm okay with that, it will be easier on her, and I'm confident that the words my dad and I spoke will make a difference.

It's been excruciating waiting for the DA to call us back once the judge has a decision. Plus, Kinsey's friends have been coming up to us nonstop. Today almost seems as hard as her funeral with all of the people that we are forced to talk to. But finally things have settled down and I'm so glad it's almost over. Arion and my dad went to grab us coffees while I sit with my mom.

The hallway is quiet; her hand is wrapped comfortably around mine.

"Bain, I love you," she says.

"I love you too, Mom."

"I'm proud of you for today. I'm sorry I couldn't get up there and speak for her."

"Thanks, Mom. And no need to apologize. I

followed my gut like you did and there's nothing wrong with that."

She smiles at me and I look to my left, catching sight of Arion and my dad as they approach. They are in deep conversation, both looking content. Before they reach us, they stop and hug. My mom squeezes my hand and then all at once our peaceful world is interrupted.

"The judge is ready," the DA says, holding the door open for us. This is the moment we've all been waiting for. My dad sets our coffees down on the bench where my mom and I were. We all make our way back into the courtroom.

We take our seats and then have to watch Anthony get brought back in. My body tenses again, seeing him. I wish he were being sentenced to life in prison or to death. Not twelve to twenty years. Regardless of what he gets, it will be hard to feel satisfied.

The judge isn't but a minute behind him. Order is called in the court, and then as we take our seats again, the judge calls Anthony up to the bench and asks him if he has anything to say. His response, "No ma'am."

The judge shakes her head and then begins to read the sentence. "Mr. Eldridge, the charges against you are severe, you do realize that?'"

He nods his head.

"So you're sure there is nothing that you would like to say?"

"Correct," he responds.

"On the charge of tampering with evidence, I hereby sentence you to seven years. On the charge of kidnapping in the first degree, I hereby sentence you to the maximum penalty allowed under your plea deal with the State of New Jersey, which is twenty years, and for first degree murder, you are sentenced to another twenty years."

"What?" he shouts. "That's not part of the plea deal."

"Order! Order in the court," the judge yells, banging her gavel. A police officer goes to Anthony reminding him that he needs to be quiet.

"Your Honor, I apologize for my client's outburst," his attorney says. "But the plea deal Mr. Eldridge took was for a maximum twenty-year sentence.

"Yes, sir, it was. And with 76A, the New Jersey law that recently passed, with any plea deal in this state an inmate takes, the judge has the right to punish based on the charges as a whole, or individually. Anthony, you took a young woman's life. You do understand that, don't you?"

"Uhhh…yes, ma'am."

"Then you really have no basis to argue. In some cases murderers are sentenced to death. In my opinion, you're getting off lucky. You'll be out of here by the time you're seventy. That sentence is nothing compared to the life you robbed Kinsey Adams of."

Hearing the judge say those words allow a rush of relief to flow through me. For the first time in almost a year, when I think about my sister, I finally feel like I can breathe again. Him being sentenced will most certainly not bring her back, but I do feel deep in my heart that today justice was served.

CHAPTER 21

-Nate-

"Are you enjoying yourself?" Nash asks me.

I knock back a swig of my beer and look around at all of the people gathered together for his birthday. His girl put together a pretty sweet party and with alcohol coursing through my system, I feel pretty good. "Yeah, this is great," I tell him.

He sits next to me on the couch and says, "Thanks for coming. I know it's not your scene, but considering everything you're doing for me, it's good to have you here."

"Thanks for dragging my ass out."

"Any time," he says raising his bottle to me. I do the same and we cheers. "Listen, I know you're not over Arion, but see that girl over there?" He points to a group of girls dancing.

"Which one?" I ask.

"The redhead. She was talking to my girl about you."

"And?"

"She thinks you're hot."

"Well, good for her."

"Come on, don't be such a bitch," he says jokingly.

"I'm not, she's just not my type."

"Have a few more beers and she will be, hell, any of the girls here will be with enough alcohol."

I shake my head listening to his absurd comment. I'm not about to get drunk in order to hook up with some chick. If I'm going to hook up with someone I want them to be a ten and I damn well want to remember it. Nash checks my beer, then hits me in the back of the head teasingly. "I'm gonna get us a few more brews."

Sitting back I watch the group of girls dance. One in particular is cute. She's blonde and reminds me of Arion. I watch her move, noticing how free she is. Arms in the air, long, blonde hair all wild and messy. Fuck, I'm horny. Maybe it's the alcohol, or her. Then she glances at me and I hold my stare. Normally I would look away, but something about her intrigues me.

She points to her friend, the redhead gesturing that she likes me and I shake my head pointing back at her. She turns her finger on herself, with a bright red face and I nod my head.

She takes her hands and weaves them into her hair turning away from me and begins to dance some more. It's like she is putting on a show, for me. Her friend is good and wasted, by her moves you can see she would be fun, but she looks like perhaps too many fun times have come her way. *No, thank you.*

Nash passes me my beer as he stands talking to a group of people.

I don't bother looking at him for long. Instead my eyes are on the blonde. She keeps looking at me as she moves and I love how my body responds to her. Everything is hot, from my head to my toes. That includes my cock, blood rushes to it, causing it to bulge in my pants.

She turns to me and gestures that I follow her, getting up I grab my crutches and make my way behind her. I make sure to keep a little distance between us, but my eyes are always on her sweet ass in a pair of tight jeans. She turns into the bathroom and I hesitate for half of a second, because of my leg, but then I envision her dancing for me and I keep going.

She's waiting for me, leaning on the wall with her arms crossed over her chest. The second I walk in, she moves, closing and locking the door behind me. "Hi," she says.

"Hey," I respond and remove my crutches, resting them against the wall, while I prop my body up on the sink. "You know if Trish knew I was in here with you, she'd be pissed as fuck."

"Well, good for Trish," I tell her. "I don't even know her, plus she's not my type."

"But I am?" she questions, stepping to me, pressing our bodies closely together.

"You are."

"So are you," she says, wrapping her arms around me and looking in my eyes.

Then without warning, I kiss her. Going right in for her soft, pink lips. She moans in response moving her hands to my hair. Our mouths become a tangled mess. Not only does she kiss like Arion, but she also tastes like her.

Taking my hands, I cup her breasts through the thin fabric of her t-shirt. With my eyes tightly shut, I imagine that I am in this moment with Arion. She kisses me harder and I'm rewarded with her two nipples as they pucker for me.

Trailing my hands down I grab the bottom of her shirt pulling it over her head. She unclasps her bra and the instant that she is topless, I pull away, taking a good look at her perfect tits.

It's been too long since I've seen a pair of these, or felt them for that matter. Reaching up I caress both of them. She surprises me by reaching into my pants while we get lost in another kiss. I can't help but let out a moan when her warm hand makes contact with my aching cock. She's aggressive just like Arion and I love that.

She smiles unbuttoning my jeans and kneels in front of me. I watch what she is doing and it doesn't take her but half of a second to pull my cock out. She jerks the skin of my shaft and already I want to blow.

"Can I suck you?" she asks.

"By all means," I respond. She takes me into her mouth, hard and ready. The tightness of her lips is really something else. Her eyes are locked on mine as she moves. She has the bluest of eyes and I think that is where the resemblance to Arion lies. I can't help but reach down with one of my hands and tug on her nipple. While my other hand has to brace my weight against the countertop.

I love that she doesn't care about my leg, I actually feel comfortable with her, which is strange considering I don't even know her name. Briefly she stops, still pushing and pulling my cock with her firm grip. Then she puts not one, but both of my balls into her mouth swirling around and around with her expert tongue. It takes everything I have to stay quiet, fuck it feels good. Then she drags her tongue up my shaft. Looking down at her, I know the second she sucks me again, I'm going to explode. And explode I do. Releasing her hand she takes me deep and I grunt like an animal, releasing the best orgasm I've had in a long time. As I drench her mouth with my cum, she keeps her movements steady...and slow.

Finally she pulls away and stands before me. "Fuck, that was amazing," I tell her, wishing more than anything that I was in this moment with Arion.

She begins to unbutton her pants and I can't believe she wants to bang now. Reaching over, I help her and she steps closer to me. Then someone knocks on the door and we both freeze. "Andrea? You in there?"

Fuck, my boyfriend. She mouths to me putting her head in her hand and shakes it back and forth. Sonofabitch.

"Nah man, I'm just pissing," I tell him.

"You sure? Her friends said she came in here."

"I'm fucking sure, check the upstairs bathroom."

Reaching behind me I turn the water on. It gets quiet and I assume he left. Andrea drops to the floor and looks under the door. Looking up at me she places her finger over her mouth and stays right where she is. Looking down at her, I can't believe myself. I guess this is one way to work towards getting over Arion.

CHAPTER 22

-Arion-

"Hey baby," I answer the phone, picking up a basket of laundry. "How was practice?"

"It was interesting and long. I'm so glad it's over."

"Oh, me too, I miss you."

"I miss you. So I was thinking we could eat out tonight, what do you think?"

"Sure, I'm finishing up the laundry now, so I haven't even thought of dinner."

"Great, I'll pick you up in thirty. I love you, Arion."

"I love you too."

We hang up and my stomach feels uneasy. There was something off with Bain's tone. I'm not sure what it was, but it was there. Crap, maybe he is going to propose tonight.

Glancing in our closet, I decide to keep it

simple and put on a pair of black, tight pants with an oversized, teal, sheer, button-down top. I pair my outfit with Bain's favorite heels. Looking in the mirror, I'm ready to head out. Guy is sleeping peacefully on his bed next to the fireplace, so I decide to leave him undisturbed and hope the decision doesn't bite me in the ass when we get home. He's been getting into some trouble lately, but I decide to give him the chance.

I go downstairs and wait for Bain. The second that Herbert sees me exit the elevator a huge grin spreads across his face.

"How are you Ms. Arion?" he asks in his ever-proper tone.

"I'm good, how are you, Herbert?"

"Enjoying each breath that God blesses me with, what more could I ask for?"

"I guess nothing. I'm glad to hear you're doing well. I hate to run, but Bain just pulled up." Outside I see Carl's black town car, Herbert opens the door for me and out comes Bain. Messy hair, jeans, and a button-down dress shirt which he has rolled the sleeves up on showing off his sexy tattoos. He closes the door and spots me as I head right towards him.

"Jesus, is this a dream?" he says engulfing me in his huge hold.

"Mmmmm," I respond breathing him in. He smells of heaven, it absolutely takes my breath away.

"God, I missed you," he says burying his nose in my hair one more time.

"Me too."

"We should get going. I made reservations at your favorite restaurant."

"How did you know I was craving it today?"

"I just knew."

We get into the car and Carl says, "Hi Arion."

"Hi," I respond, then get lost in Bain's mouth as it finds my throat. He leaves kisses all over me. Soft, warm, affectionate kisses, and I give in closing my eyes. Then I remember Carl is in the front seat and pull away. Bain groans in protest looking at me through hooded lids.

"Later," I whisper into his ear.

He accepts my offer, although I can tell he doesn't want to.

"My mom called today," he says, doing a complete one eighty.

"How is she?"

"She's okay, she wanted to see if we wanted to go to Costa Rica with them before the season starts."

"Really? Why there?"

"My dad has a conference. What do you think?"

"I would love to."

"Good, I'll tell her. What did you do today?" he asks.

"Not much…worked, laundry, and cleaned a little. I think I got you a sweet deal with Gatorade."

"Heck yeah, baby, that's awesome."

"Here we are," Carl interrupts. "I'll get the door for you guys."

Bain exits the car reaching for my hand. I take it and keep my eyes on his, the way I always do in these situations. Looking around, there are just normal patrons on the street, and no one notices us, it feels so good.

We head inside and get seated right away. Bain requested our normal table…it's nice and quiet and tucked away in the back of the restaurant with a beautiful view of the Hudson.

"You look stunning tonight," he says.

"Thank you, baby. You're looking pretty

good yourself."

"Thanks. So how was Guy today?" he asks.

"He was good, minus barking at his shadow all day. I really think we should consider moving somewhere with a yard."

"I know. I do too. That's part of why I wanted to take you out to dinner."

The waiter approaches and Bain orders a bottle of Don P. There must be something going on, considering that Don is a few hundred dollars a bottle.

"All right, spill it," I order him to tell me.

"Can we wait for the champagne?"

"No," I blurt out a little too loud.

"Fine. I know I've been on the fence lately about moving, but that's because this whole trade thing has been up in the air. I didn't want to make a move 'til I knew what was going to happen, and today...I found out."

"And?"

"We have to move. The Nets traded me to Miami. I'm going to buy you the biggest and most beautiful house on the water that you could imagine. Baby, please tell me you're happy."

"Bain, I couldn't care less about the house and all of that. For me, it's about being together.

If Miami is where we're going next, then lets do it. Just tell me when I should start packing."

A huge smile spans his face. "I have a physical down there the day after tomorrow, so I think we are going to have to get going – fast."

"What about Guy?"

"He can come too. Baby, you know Guy is part of the family, we'll stick together and stay happy, okay?"

The waiter comes back with our champagne and pours us two glasses. "Would you like to start with any appetizers tonight?" he asks.

"Can we do two orders of the scallops?"

"Sure, I'll get those in right away."

I lift my drink and Bain does the same. He looks at me with a little uncertainty in his eyes. I want to wash all his worry away. "To our future, and Miami."

He nods his head and we clink glasses. Then he leans in kissing me hard before I can even take a sip.

"So you're really okay with moving to Florida?"

"Yes, I don't care where we go. I really have no reason to stay in Jersey. My whole life I've searched for a place to belong and I've finally found it. For a while I thought that was in Jersey with Aubrey, but not anymore. My place is in your heart, with you, so it doesn't matter where we live. I'm more concerned with how you feel about it."

"I'm gonna miss my parents, but ultimately, I'm relieved. It'll be a fresh start away from everything I've been through here with Kinsey and the case. It's taken a toll on me and I feel like a move will be good. Especially with that bastard being sentenced."

"I agree, it is the perfect time. Did the Nets say why they are trading you when you were their top pick and they put so much money out there for you."

"They said that their organization is going in a different direction."

"Well, whatever that means. If they don't want you, there are obviously teams out there that do."

"That's exactly what I thought."

"Do you know anyone in Miami?"

"I actually went to school with one of their centers. His name is Trenton, he was there the night I met you. You'll like him – he's funny as fuck."

The waiter comes back setting down our scallops and asks, "Have you had a chance to look over the menu?"

"Uhhh, not yet," Bain tells him.

"Well, take your time. Please let me know if I can answer any questions."

"We will."

I look down at the delicious plate in front of us. It smells amazing and I can't help myself from digging in. "You're so crazy," Bain tells me.

"I know, so you better grab some if you want any scallops of your own."

We eat and talk, both of us surprisingly excited over Miami. The warm weather will be nice, and this change of pace I believe came at the right time.

"What are you gonna get to eat, babe?"

"The lobster and steak, you?"

"Same."

We laugh and then Bain orders our food. Looking down at the clean plates, I probably ate more scallops, than I needed to, but they were divine.

"Should I book us flights to Miami?"

"Probably, I was gonna see if my parents would keep Guy while we went."

"Okay." My stomach starts to cramp and I regret gorging on the food right away. I place my hand over it to try and stop it.

"Are you all right?" Bain asks me.

"Yeah, I just think I ate too much. I'm gonna go to the restroom."

"Okay, baby."

I smile the best I can to reassure Bain that I'm okay. I'm sure some cold water on my face will help. I walk into the restroom, but lose it. Everything goes out the window. *Fuck that.* The smell nauseates me so bad that I run into a stall and get sick, before I can even close the door behind me.

As I kneel on the floor breathing heavily with my long hair in my hands, I notice that the smell which made me sick is some sort of perfume or air freshener. It's fucking gross. Thinking about it makes me sick again to the point of dry heaving.

Exhausted and famished, I finally pull myself off of the floor. Looking in the mirror, my eyes are red and my face is blotchy. Those scallops definitely did not agree with me. I wash my hands and splash some water on my face. Making my way back to Bain, he stands right away, coming towards me.

"What happened?"

"I don't know. I was fine, then there was this smell in the bathroom and I lost it. I threw everything up."

"Oh, baby, I'm sorry. Let's get you home."

I nod my head and Bain waves the waiter over. "Can we get our check please?"

"Sure, but your meals?"

"My girlfriend just got sick from your food. So we'll pass."

"Oh, please accept our apologies. The meal is on us, Mr. Adams."

"Thanks," Bain says and grabs my hand, walking us towards the front doors.

"Carl," Bain barks into the phone. "We're ready." He hangs up and looks at me. "Are you sure that you're okay?"

"Yeah, I feel better."

He kisses my forehead and we wait outside for Carl. The events that just took place swirl around my head. Why did I get so sick? It's not like me at all.

Then someone walks by with a cigarette and I inhale the scent. What once was my favorite habit gives me that same nauseous feeling. I know right away that it wasn't the food.

I take a few deep breaths to calm my stomach and count back to my last period. "Fuck," I blurt out.

"What? Are you going to get sick again?"

I shake my head. "No. No, Bain...I think I might be pregnant."

He smiles ear to ear and asks me, "Really?"

"I think so."

"Why?"

"My period is late and the way everything smells is making me feel strange."

We get into the back of Carl's car and Bain asks him, "Carl, will you stop at a CVS?"

"Yes, sir, I will."

"Why are you smiling at me like that?" I ask him.

He has the biggest grin on his face. "Arion, I don't know how you feel about kids, I mean, we've never talked about it. But just imagine," he says placing his hand over my stomach.

I slap it away. Is he out of his goddamn mind? "No, Bain!"

"Here you go. I'll wait here," Carl says.

Bain practically drags me out of the car. I'm in shock. What the fuck are we doing? It's not possible. I take my pill every day and I don't miss it. I never have. This can't be happening right now.

"Which one do we buy?" Bain asks me, looking at the shelves of pregnancy tests.

I shake my head and he kisses my cheek, grabbing the most expensive one.

"Wanna take the test here?" he asks me after we check out.

"No, I'm not going to find out if we are pregnant in the bathroom of a fucking CVS."

With that shit-eating grin plastered on his face, we get back in the car. I look up and sense Carl has caught on to what we are doing as Bain reads the back of the box. "Don't you say a word, Carl," I snap at him.

"Not a word, ma'am."

"Put that back in the bag," I gripe at Bain before we get out of the car at the condo. Both of us race across the lobby, my sudden sickness gone. When we enter the apartment, Guy looks up at us like we are two loons as we run into the bathroom.

"What do I do with it?" I ask him.

"Just pee on it, I guess."

"Maybe we should wait and see if I get sick again. I'm sure it was just the food."

"Arion, your period is late. We have to fly to Miami soon. You're doing this."

I nod my head taking the test from him and go to the toilet. After I'm done I hand it back to him and we stand there waiting. The room around us is as still as a movie on pause. Guy comes into the room and sits next to Bain. He scratches the top of his head while we stare at this ridiculous stick that could change our lives forever.

"I know we've never talked about it, but regardless what it says, Arion, I want kids. I really do."

Then the result on the screen is displayed, *Pregnant*. I blink a few times and watch Bain drop to his knees. He lifts my shirt and begins kissing my stomach. I stand frozen, a tad bit in shock. Tears flow from my eyes, watching him. Bain on his knees in front of me like this is nothing I've ever seen.

He presses his lips to my stomach and whispers something, then says, "Stay here."

I nod my head knowing in this moment that I couldn't move if I wanted to. Guy follows Bain and I see him rummaging in his dresser. Then he comes to me, stopping in the doorway of the bathroom for half a second. He takes a deep breath and looks down at the box in his hand.

My hand flies to my mouth, and he kneels down on one knee in front of me. I reach for his hair, my breathing is getting heavy and he takes my hand placing the ring box in it. As we are immobile in this moment, it's as if the room around us spins. Everything moves so fast, except for us.

"Arion, you have made me the happiest man in the world on so many different levels. You challenge me, you defy me, you motivate me to be a better person, and most of all, you love me unconditionally. I bought this ring a while ago and knew I would ask you when the moment was right. Well…that moment is now. You are going to be the mother of my child and you complete me on every level humanly possible. I love you more than anything. Would you do me the honor of becoming my wife? Will you marry me?"

"Yes. Yes. Yes," I instantly repeat.

He opens the box, and inside is a beautiful, round-cut diamond ring in the most exquisite setting. It's laced and sprinkled with so many diamonds that I can't fathom it on my finger. Bain pulls it out and slides it on me. It fits perfectly.

EPILOGUE

-Bain-

9 months later

"Baby?" I yell for Arion.

I get no response, but then again, this house is huge, so it is hard to hear. We are finally all settled in Miami. Things are comfortable and we both love it here. I finished my first NBA season and won Rookie of the Year. I led my team in scoring and assists making the playoffs. We got knocked out in the first round but still it was a great year. Now it's time to focus on getting ready for our baby boy, who is due any day now.

"Baby," I call her again and head up stairs.

"I'm in here." I can tell right away she is in the baby's room. *Of course she is.*

"What are you doing in here?"

"Laundry."

"How many clothes does the kid need?"

"A lot. Look at this," she says, holding up an itty-bitty Miami Heat jersey with my number and name on it.

"Holy shit, that's awesome. Where did you get it?"

"Your mom mailed it to us."

"She's the best. How are you feeling?" I ask her, sitting on the floor in front of the ottoman she has her feet on. I begin to rub them as she starts to talk.

"I'm cramping a lot. The Braxton Hicks contractions haven't stopped all day, but I guess it's my body just getting ready."

"I know. I can't believe he'll be here any day."

"God, I know, time really flies."

"Yeah, it does. Have you decided on a name yet, beautiful?"

Her face scrunches and she puts her hand over her stomach. Her wedding set gleams, almost blinding me. We got married in Costa Rica when we went with my parents right after I proposed. She didn't want to be showing in the pictures and I just wanted her to be my wife, so

Costa Rice was perfect.

"Are you okay?" I ask her.

"Yeah, they stopped. I was thinking we could name him after my dad, Aaron and I was thinking his middle name could be Kins for Kinsey. Aaron Kins Adams."

"I love it."

"Really?"

"Yeah."

"Good. Now, hang these up for me."

"Yes, drill sergeant."

"Don't call me that. I just don't want the baby to come home to a house that is in shambles."

I can't help but chuckle at her. "This place is far from shambles...it's seven thousand square feet of prime waterfront real estate," he says with a huge grin on his face.

"I do love it here."

"Me too."

I sit back down and rub her feet. "God, that feels good," she says.

"Yeah, what about this?" I ask her, kissing the top of her foot, then I begin trailing kisses up her calf and thigh.

"Mmm, I like that too," she says.

Of course she does, I know what she likes. Not stopping my kisses, I move higher and higher up her body 'til I reach her panties. She's only wearing them and one of my t-shirts. Moving the shirt out of the way, I pull her panties to the side.

God, she drives me wild. She always has and I know she always will. It's her scent...there is something about the way any part of her smells that gets me going. Especially here. She scoots forward and I dip my tongue between her wet slit, tasting her sweetness. My body almost convulses by how good it is. Arion moans, gripping the arms of the plush grey chair that she's sitting in.

Her noises make me move my tongue and mouth that much harder and faster. God, I want her, my whole body aches for hers. To be inside of her, so I slow my movements and lift her out of the chair. Even pregnant, she barely weighs anything. I move on a mission to make love to my wife.

Her arms are around my neck and head against my chest. My eyes move to her stomach, I can't help but stare there, to the place where our son is growing so comfortably. As I step foot on the plush, white carpet of our room, I set her down, pulling the t-shirt she's wearing over her head. Staring at her in just a pair of panties like this, takes my breath away. I absolutely married the sexiest woman in the world.

-*Arion*-

Bain's expression is carnal. He's a machine and I love it when he looks at me like this. He has so many sides to him and the beast that he is in bed turns me on like nothing else. Moving my hand, I slide it under the thin lace of my underwear and pull them down. He kneels in front of me and helps them all the way down my legs, so I don't have to bend. I don't think I'll ever get tired of him pampering me. My heart races because I know what we are in for is going to satisfy us both, to the fullest.

"On the bed," he orders, turning me around so I'm headed in the right direction. I walk with adrenaline in my veins and excitement running through my system. Bain's hands guide me and when I reach the bed, I start to lie on my back, but he stops me.

"On your knees. I want your ass up."

Grabbing the back of his head, I turn and kiss him. He holds on to my body and kisses me back, giving me so much passion and love. Then I crawl away, staying on my knees like he wants. I can sense he is getting undressed himself and turn to see the last of his clothes hit the floor. His cock is hard, and I can't wait for him to be inside of me. I don't know what it is about being pregnant, but my sex drive is on a whole other level. He kneels up on the bed and moves to me on his knees. His breathing is heavy and when he reaches me he doesn't waste another second before he grabs his cock and guides himself inside of me.

"Oh fuck," I moan. The feeling is so good.

Slowly he teases me, nuzzling himself all the way inside of me, then taking his hands, he grips my ass pulling my cheeks apart and begins to move. He's so gentle moving in and out of me.

"Christ, I love your pussy," he tells me.

I moan in return, bracing my weight the best that I can. Bain stays slow with his movements and asks, "Is this okay?"

"Yes," I respond. My body is now covered from head to toe in bliss. Everything he does makes me hot. He picks up speed a little and the faster he moves the louder I get. Dropping my head down low, I know this won't last long. My body is too close. But I hang on, knowing that soon everything will be different. We will no longer have our time together to fuck whenever we please like this, because baby Aaron is going to flip our world upside down.

"Fuck," Bain yells, and I feel his cock harden even more inside of me. I know he is close and I stop fighting my orgasm. I push myself up so I am just kneeling; my back is to his front and we wrap our arms around each other.

As he moves himself into me so deeply, my body convulses. Everything quakes and I close my eyes tightly, then…my release. It hits me hard. My orgasm washes over me and I scream. Letting Bain take me out of this world. He grunts along with me, still being as gentle as ever. *Goddamn, he's something else.*

Once our bodies settle, he lays us down on our sides. His hand rests comfortably on my heart, on his heart. It really is no longer mine. It belongs to him. Lying with Bain in silence like this is the best place in the world. My body relaxes and I give in to the inevitable sleep that I need. Then out of nowhere, it happens. I sit up, looking between my legs and I know it's time. "Fuck, my water broke."

-Nate-

"Rookie of the Year, Bain Adams, has welcomed his first child into the world. Sources close to the couple say both baby and mom are doing well," the tabloid reporter says through the TV. I grab the remote, pissed that my mom left this shit on and turn it off angrily.

With news like that, I feel like the last thread of the hold I'd been grasping on to with Arion has just completely slipped away. Taking my shoes off, I grab everything I need to make a protein smoothie. My workout today was brutal. Lately, I've been pushing myself beyond my normal limits. Partly to replace the pain of the loss I feel for Arion with something else, and also I just want to get into the best shape of my life.

It feels good to know that I am getting there, slowly, but surely. I mean, last I'd checked I was up to a hundred and ninety pounds and it's all muscle. My phone rings as I start to wash some of the fruit I'm using. I wipe my hand on a towel then grab it. I can tell it's the gym.

"Hello," I answer, resting the phone between my ear and shoulder.

"Hi Nate, it's Amanda. I'm really sorry to bug you, I tried to call Nash first but he didn't answer."

"It's okay. What's up?" Amanda is one of our personal trainers and does a few of the classes we offer.

"This is going to sound really dumb, but I twisted my ankle working out after my shift. It's really swollen, so I'm going to have it looked at. But I'm not sure that I can open in the morning. I mean, I'll—"

I cut her off, "I got you. Don't even worry about it. Just take care of yourself and let me know what the doctor says."

"Thanks," she responds.

"Any time."

We hang up and I start the blender. In the

distance I hear a bang, but with the blender going, I'm not sure if that's really what I heard. Once my drink is all finished, I pour it into a cup and head upstairs. When I got home my mom was sleeping, so I'm sure it wasn't her.

But to be sure I head towards her room. Quietly I open the door, making sure I don't wake her. Peeking in, she's not in her bed like she was before.

My heart starts to race. "Ma," I yell, but get no response. I go into the bathroom next to her room. The second I take in the scene before me, I drop the cup out of my hand as nothing but sheer horror flashes before my eyes...

FOR MY READERS

You did it! You patiently waited, and finally, after what seemed like forever, found out what happened to Bain and Arion. I need to give each and every one of you a big thank you. I know at the end of *Every Soul,* you were mad at me, and I said it then and I'll say it now, "That's okay." *Every Soul* was not intended to give Bain and Arion their HEA, but *Every Heart* was. I know with this book, you were freaking out, wondering who she was going to choose and wondering what was going to happen. But throughout the journey and all that wondering, did you really think that Arion wouldn't pick Bain? Like he said, "I really think if you follow your heart, then we'll end up together."

So with that said, what's next? Well, our boy, Nate, needs his own book, wouldn't you say? He's beefed up and toned, now he just needs a lady. The problem: all he wants is Arion. Clearly he can't have her, because Bain, Arion, and baby Aaron are happy and far, far away in Miami. My point being, *Every Love* is all Nate, no cliffhanger, I promise. :)

After *Every Love*, I'm diving back into the Life. Destiny. Fate. series to give Liam his own book in *Skepticism*, then we move on to Lincoln's book in *Optimism*. So if you haven't read any of the Life. Destiny. Fate. books, you so need to. They are HOT and packed full of steamy sex!

ACKNOWLEDGEMENTS

To be sitting here writing this and to have completed my fifth book is simply…mind blowing. Someone please wake me up, because this must be a dream come true.

Anyone who knows me, knows I can't do what I do without my partner in crime, Mr. Prezident! So as always, I must start my thanks to him. Thank you for planning these stories with me and for making sure that they come to life beautifully. Your craft is amazing, and as I've said before, I will always keep it to myself. Not only do you push me with my writing and are brutally honest in doing so, but you love and support me along the way. Damn, I'm lucky, so lucky. Thank you, baby, for simply…everything. I love you.

Lisa, Lisa, Lisa, shall we agree to disagree? In this one we did, and I have to say it was a first. Normally, I am a good student, I always listen and take what you have to say into consideration, but with *Every Heart*, I knew my readers would kill me if I dragged out the break-up. So, I had to stick to my guns. Now I'm not saying I won, but I recently had lunch with a blogger and one of the first things she said when we sat down was, "Thank you for having Arion make her decision so early." Enough about that. Thank you for always having my back and for supporting my vision with my stories. I love how well we work together and how we laugh at the same things. I can't believe we have completed four books together, and I'm so happy to do so many more.

Leticia, thank you for knocking this baby out so quickly. You are so great at what you do and I appreciate it. I can't believe we've completed another book together. You have become such a dear friend to me and for that I am grateful.

To my Pimpettes and Book Club, I love you all! You support me in the most unimaginable ways. Thank you for reading and loving my stories, for pushing me to be a better writer, and most of all, for your honesty. Thank you for yelling at me and telling me how you really feel.

Lydia with HEA Bookshelf, thank you for helping me organize both a successful cover reveal and blog tour. And to every single blogger that has helped me along the way, thank you! As an indie author, what I do would not be possible without all of you. I wish I could name each and every one of you, but I'd leave someone out and that wouldn't be fair. But please know: every tag or blog post or mention of my books and my work makes me so happy.